He Leaned In, His Mouth Close To Her Ear, His Breath On Her Face.

She held her arms to her side to stop herself from doing something monumentally stupid. But she suspected that it was already too late. And just as she decided to give in, the phone started to ring.

"I should get that," she said, slipping out from under his arm and dashing to the cordless on the table.

She glanced over her shoulder at Ethan, where he leaned casually against the door, watching her. She couldn't think straight when those smoky eyes were fixed her way.

This was it. She could leave now and put an end to this. For tonight anyway, and possibly forever. Or she could stay. With Ethan. Knowing exactly what that would mean.

This time, it wouldn't end with just a kiss.

Dear Reader,

Welcome to book two of my ROYAL SEDUCTIONS series! The story of Ethan Rafferty, the king's illegitimate half brother, and the queen's personal assistant, Lizzy Pryce. (And if you didn't already know, book one of the series, *The King's Convenient Bride,* is also available *now* from Silhouette Desire.)

Never have I met a couple so different, yet so perfectly suited. Convincing them of that, however, is another story. They are so darned sure they have it all figured out that they can't see what is so obviously right in front of them. And even when they do, stubborn as they are, they won't let themselves believe it's real.

I hope you enjoy their journey!

See you next time for the third installment, Princess Sophie's story, coming soon from Silhouette Desire.

Best,

Michelle

THE
ILLEGITIMATE
PRINCE'S
BABY

MICHELLE CELMER

Published by Silhouette Books
America's Publisher of Contemporary Romance

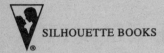

SILHOUETTE BOOKS

ISBN-13: 978-0-373-76877-6
ISBN-10:   0-373-76877-X

THE ILLEGITIMATE PRINCE'S BABY

Copyright © 2008 by Michelle Celmer

Visit Silhouette Books at www.eHarlequin.com

Printed in U.S.A.

Books by Michelle Celmer

Silhouette Desire

The Millionaire's Pregnant Mistress #1739
The Secretary's Secret #1774
Best Man's Conquest #1799
*The King's Convenient Bride #1876
*The Illegitimate Prince's Baby #1877

Silhouette Intimate Moments

Running on Empty #1342
Out of Sight #1398

Silhouette Special Edition

Accidentally Expecting #1847

*Royal Seductions

MICHELLE CELMER

Bestselling author Michelle Celmer lives in southeastern Michigan with her husband, their three children, two dogs and two cats. When she's not writing or busy being a mom, you can find her in the garden or curled up with a romance novel. And if you twist her arm real hard you can usually persuade her into a day of power shopping.

Michelle loves to hear from readers. Visit her Web site at: www.michellecelmer.com, or write her at P.O. Box 300, Clawson, MI 48017.

To my newest great-nephew, Lucas Callum,
who couldn't be a cuter, sweeter little guy.

One

She couldn't believe she was really doing this.

Lizzy Pryce climbed the palace steps, feeling as if she was walking into a dream. Through the open, gilded double doors she could see a throng of guests milling about the foyer, dressed in sparkling gowns and tailored tuxedos. Waiters carried trays of mouth-watering hors d'oeuvres and champagne in delicate crystal flutes. From the ballroom she could hear the orchestra—the one she herself had chosen—playing a waltz. She could just imagine the couples dancing, swirling across the floor, so graceful and light they looked as though they hovered an inch above ground.

Everything in her wanted to turn around and run, but she'd come this far. She had to see this through.

Gathering her courage, she approached the guard posted at the door and handed him her invitation. Normally palace employees were strictly forbidden from attending royal parties, but this was the gala celebrating Morgan Isle's five hundredth anniversary. The party of the century. And because she held one of the highest positions—the queen's personal assistant—her name had been included on the guest list.

Her married name, that is. She didn't want people to recognize her. It was silly, but just for tonight, she wanted to feel as if she was one of them. The beautiful people. She certainly looked the part.

The golden-blond hair that she normally kept pinned back and fastened primly at the base of her neck now tumbled in loose tendrils across her shoulders and down her back. She'd ditched her glasses for contacts. And she'd abandoned her usual shapeless, dull—but proper—business suit for the formfitting, shimmering gold, Carlos Miele gown she had rented.

At the risk of sounding arrogant, she looked damn good.

The guard compared the name on the invitation to his list then motioned her through without a second glance.

As Lizzy stepped through the door into the foyer, one by one heads began to turn her way until what must have been a hundred pairs of curious eyes fixed right on her.

Don't get too excited, she told herself. They're only looking because they don't know who you are.

But she couldn't help noticing some of those looks, particularly the male ones, conveyed more appreciation than curiosity.

Head held high, she made her way through the crowd to the ballroom, nodding graciously and returning polite greetings with people she'd only read about in the papers or seen on television. Heads of state, Hollywood film stars and business moguls.

She was way out of her league. The value of the jewelry alone would probably feed an entire Third World country for a year. She hadn't even made it out of the foyer and she was a nervous wreck.

Lizzy, you have just as much right to be here as anyone else.

She swiped a glass of champagne from a passing waiter and took a generous swallow, the bubbles tickling her nose. She was only a few steps from the ballroom doors.

Just do it, walk in, her conscience taunted. So she took a deep breath and forced her feet to propel her forward.

Stepping through the doors and into the ballroom was like entering some ethereal, fairy-tale fantasyland where everything sparkled and shimmered. Handsome couples swished across the dance floor while others congregated in small groups, sipping their champagne and chatting, nibbling on decadent treats.

It was just as she had imagined. And for an instant she felt swept away.

"Excuse me," a male voice said from behind her,

and the first thing that struck her was the very distinct American accent.

Taking another fortifying sip of her champagne, she turned and nearly spit it right back out.

Not only was he American, he was the Prince of Morgan Isle. Illegitimate half brother to the king. Half brother-in-law to the queen, Lizzy's boss.

Georgeous, rich, undeniably arrogant but charming to a fault. Of all the men who could have approached her, the one who was by far the most off limits, did.

"I don't believe we've met," he said.

She thought he was toying with her, then she realized, by the look on his handsome, chiseled face and the curiosity in his charcoal-gray eyes, he honestly had no idea who she was. And why would he? The few times he had passed her in the halls of the palace, he hadn't given her more than a fleeting glance. And why would he? She was an employee.

"I don't believe we have," she said.

He offered his hand. "Ethan Rafferty."

When she took it, instead of shaking her hand, he bent at the waist and brushed a gentle, and dare she say seductive, kiss across the top. No big surprise there. She didn't know a lot about the prince, only that he was a confirmed bachelor and a shameless womanizer. She had overheard the queen countless times commenting on the rather scandalous state of his very public personal life. She had also heard the king complain of Ethan's lack of respect for their royal customs and policies. Which would explain why Ethan was dressed in a tux and not the royal uniform. The dark hair was slicked back away from his face. A face that bore an uncanny resemblance to his brother's.

Ethan's recent acceptance into the royal fold, and his new business partnership with the family, was all anyone at the palace talked about these days.

Though she couldn't deny that seeing him like this, watching the way his eyes raked over her, was the tiniest bit thrilling. He was the epitome of male perfection, and he smelled absolutely delicious. Just as a prince and a multimillionaire should, she supposed.

Her ex-husband had been gorgeous, too, and smelled just as nice, though he was lacking the millions of dollars or the motivation to earn even a fraction of that. And like the prince he was also an arrogant, womanizing, philandering dolt.

But because Ethan *was* royalty, she curtsied and replied, "It's a pleasure, Your Highness."

He actually cringed. "I'm not much into titles. I prefer just Ethan."

She was pretty sure that if he knew who she really was, he wouldn't be so gracious. And while this had been kind of fun, it was time to move on. Find a guest who wasn't quite so far out of her league. And against policy. Palace employees were strictly forbidden from intimate relationships with the royal family.

"Well, it was nice to meet you." She nodded and curtsied—force of habit—then turned and headed in the opposite direction.

"I didn't catch your name," Ethan said from behind her, and her heart sank.

Bugger. Couldn't the man take a hint? She set her empty glass on a passing waiter's tray and grabbed a fresh drink. "That's because I didn't tell you my name." She tossed the quip back over her shoulder.

"And why is that?" he asked, right beside her now.

She took a long swallow for strength. A smart person was not rude to royalty. Even though the last documented beheading had been well over two hundred years ago.

Of course, he had no idea who she was, so really, what did she have to lose? And who knew, maybe it was time someone put Mr. Wonderful in his place.

"Because you're not my type," she told him, and he had the gall to laugh.

"You're a liar."

She stopped so abruptly the contents of her glass sloshed over and dripped onto her fingers. He stopped, too. "I beg your pardon?"

"Look at me," he said, spreading his arms. "What's not to love?"

She couldn't tell if he was joking or actually had such a high opinion of himself. Could he honestly be *that* arrogant? "I have to know, does that pathetic excuse for a pickup line actually work?"

He grinned, a sexy, playful smile that made her heart flutter. "I'll let you know in a minute."

He was adorable, and he knew it. And she knew, before she opened her mouth, that telling him her name was a very bad idea. But maybe if she did, he would lose interest and leave her alone.

"Lizzy," she told him, since everyone at work knew her strictly as Elizabeth. And instead of Pryce, the name she had switched back to before the ink was dry on the divorce papers, she used her married name. "Lizzy Sinclaire."

"Would you do me the honor of a dance, Ms. Sinclaire?"

Because she so hated that name and everything it stood for, she told him, "I prefer Lizzy."

"All right, Lizzy."

"And no, I won't dance with you. Because as I said, you're not my type."

Rather than be insulted, or discouraged, his grin widened. "I'm not asking for your hand in marriage. Just a dance. Unless…" His brow wrinkled. "Oh, I see. You don't know how to dance, do you?"

Oh, please, did he really think she would fall for his pathetic attempt at reverse psychology?

The truth was, she and her ex had taken ballroom dance classes several years ago. Only later had she learned that he'd been the one giving personal lessons to the instructor.

"You've found me out," she told him. "Now, if you would please excuse me." She spared him one last dismissive nod then turned and walked back in the direction of the foyer, chanting to herself, *Please don't let him follow me. Please don't let him follow me.*

"I could teach you," she heard him say, and cursed

under her breath. He was right back beside her, matching her step for step.

"I might step on your foot and scuff your shoe," she said.

He shrugged. "It's been stepped on before."

She stopped again and turned to him. "Why is it so important you dance with a woman who has no desire to dance with you?"

He flashed her that grin again, and she swore she could feel it all the way through to her bones. "Because the woman in question is the most captivating in the room."

Oh, man, was he good. He almost had her believing he was sincere. Ethan's words could have melted her into a puddle. Which she was sure was exactly his intention. Men like him didn't see women as people. They were conquests. A notch in the bedpost, so to speak.

She drained the last of her second glass. "I just don't think it would be a good idea."

Ethan took her empty glass and set it on the tray of the waiter who magically appeared at his side. "Please, one dance."

She didn't think a man like him used the word *please*. And there was something about it that sounded so…genuine. She could feel her resolve slip the tiniest bit. And it certainly didn't help that she was feeling a little giddy from the champagne.

All she had to do was to tell him who she was, and she was sure he would lose interest, but for some reason she couldn't make herself say the words. How often in life was a girl lucky enough to be pursued by a prince? And honestly, what harm would one little dance do? Even if someone recognized her, she could claim she was simply being polite.

"Fine," she told him. "*One* dance."

He offered her his arm and led her out to the dance floor. She glanced nervously around, noting with relief that the queen, the one person who might actually recognize her, was nowhere in sight.

Ethan took her in his arms and she experienced a delicious shiver of awareness, one she blamed on the champagne. Because in her right mind she would never feel sexually attracted to an arrogant woman-izing cad like him. She didn't care how many millions he possessed or hotel resorts he owned.

But one little dance never hurt anyone.

He led her in a waltz and she found him to be quite an accomplished dancer.

"So, you *are* a liar," he said, and she shot him a questioning look. "I think my shoes are safe."

"Your shoes?"

"This is definitely not the first time you've danced."

Caught red-handed. "No," she admitted. "It isn't."

And it obviously wasn't his first time, either. He seemed to glide, light as the air, across the floor.

"It's not so bad, is it? Dancing with me, I mean."

Not bad at all. In fact, it was so *not* bad, that when the song ended and a new one began, she didn't pull away. And still she couldn't completely relax.

One dance could easily be explained. But two? And why hadn't she told him who she was? She really *should* tell him.

"I didn't see the queen," she said. "Is she here?"

"Why, would you like to meet her?"

"No, I was just curious."

"She's probably in the parlor resting. She's expecting soon."

"I believe I had heard that." And Lizzy was grateful to know that Queen Hannah was staying off her feet, as the doctor had advised when she began to complain of regular and intense back pain. Lizzy was constantly after her to take it easy, put her feet up and relax a little. Just as she was always after Lizzy to not work so hard, to take some time off and have fun. But ten- and twelve-hour workdays were an excellent excuse to continue to ignore the fact that she had no life.

"Are you excited to become an uncle?" she asked Ethan.

He shrugged and the planes of his face hardened almost imperceptibly. "I suppose."

He didn't look excited. "You don't like kids?"

"Kids are great. It's the child's father I'm not all that crazy about."

Lizzy knew they didn't get along, but wasn't aware that Ethan harbored such a deep animosity toward the king. And she was a sucker for juicy gossip. So, when the song ended and another began, a slower melody, she pretended not to notice that their one dance had now become three.

"Sibling rivalry?" she asked, shamelessly pumping him for information. "My sisters and I certainly had our share."

"To call him a brother is a stretch. We simply have the misfortune of sharing a few chromosomes. Any familiarity stops there." He spun her around then pulled her back in, much closer than she had been before. So close she could feel the heat of his body radiating through his clothes. Close enough to make her heart do a quick back-and-forth shimmy in her chest.

She felt like a princess, whirling across the dance floor with the world's elite, as though she actually belonged here. As if she were one of them.

But it was an illusion. A fluke.

Tell him who you are, her conscience insisted, but she blocked the annoying voice out. Just a few more minutes.

One more dance, then she would walk away.

Two

Ethan had never intended to spend the entire evening with one woman, but there was something about Lizzy, something that set her apart.

It wasn't her striking beauty, at least not entirely. At a function like this, beautiful women ran in packs. She was different in a way that he couldn't quite put his finger on.

Whatever it was, the instant he'd seen her enter the ballroom, he'd known he'd had to meet her.

Excusing himself from the Hollywood starlet that had been clamoring for his attention—his third or fourth already this evening—he'd approached her. And though she'd tried to hide it, he'd seen her initial surprise when he'd introduced himself. Not unusual these days. The fact that she'd brushed him off had only intrigued him more.

It had been an awfully long time since he'd had to pursue a woman. More often than not they were fighting each other for his attention. Anything to get close to the hotel mogul and self-made millionaire. Of course, if they knew just how close he had come to losing it all, they might not be so hot on his heels.

But Lizzy seemed to genuinely dislike him, which for some twisted reason, he'd found undeniably attractive. And when he'd taken her in his arms, his reaction had been unexpected and surprisingly intense physical attraction. Another rare occurrence these days. In the past he would never pass up a night of good company and a quick roll in the hay. But lately even the most attractive of women held little or no appeal.

Which made him all the more determined to get inside her head. Under her skin. And with any luck, get her out of her clothes.

The music set ended and everyone stopped to applaud. Now that they weren't dancing, would she try to escape?

"I don't know about you," he said, "but I could use some fresh air."

She glanced toward the foyer. "I really should go."

And he should relent, but for some reason he didn't want to let her get away. "A short stroll on the balcony is all I'm asking for."

Indecision clouded her face.

"Five minutes," he cajoled.

She hesitated, then said, "Only five."

He offered his arm and she slipped hers through it. He led her to the balcony doors and added, "Ten, tops." And before she could object, they were already out the door.

The night air was cool and damp, although unusually warm for late May. Or so he'd been told. He knew little about his native country's climate and weather patterns. And honestly, he didn't care. He cared even less about the traditions and customs the king had been all but cramming down his throat lately. If he had realized all of the hassle this partnership would cost him, he might have taken his chances and stayed on his own continent. But he was in too deep to back out now. The royal family was saving him and he had to tread lightly.

He signaled a passing waiter and stole a drink from his tray. "Champagne?" he offered.

She nodded and took it from him, sipping, he noticed, much slower than the first two. He took one for himself, and walked her over to the wrought-iron railing that overlooked acres of manicured lawn, trees of every size and shape exploding with green, and in the distance, his half sister Princess Sophie's private residence.

She let go of his arm and leaned on the railing, looking out over the estate with what could only be described as longing in her eyes. "It's beautiful at night, isn't it? All the lights in the garden."

She said it as though it wasn't her first time here, and that surprised him. "You've been to the palace before?"

She blinked rapidly, as though she just realized she'd said something she shouldn't have. Revealed too much. And she seemed to choose her next words carefully. "A time or two."

"Friend or family?"

She shrugged. "Neither, really."

He studied her profile. Her features managed to be delicate but strong at the same time. Refined, but with an element of something wild and untamed.

What was going on in her head? What was she hiding? There was obviously something. And it intrigued him. "How is it, then, that you know the royal family?"

Again she took great care in her response. "I guess you could say…through business."

He leaned on the railing beside her. "What is it you do for a living?"

"It's getting colder." She shivered and rubbed her bare arms, deliberately avoiding his question.

He wasn't quite ready to go back inside, so he shrugged out of his jacket and draped it across her shoulders. The silky ribbons of her hair brushed against him and he couldn't help wondering how it would feel to tangle his fingers through it.

All in good time, he assured himself.

He turned her to face him, adjusting the lapel. "Better?"

"Much. Thank you." She looked up at him and

smiled. An honest-to-goodness, genuine smile. Her first of the night, he realized, and the result was devastating. He thought she was beautiful before, but he could see now that it was merely the tip of the iceberg.

But as abruptly as the smile formed, it disappeared, as though it suddenly occurred to her what she'd done and it was wrong somehow.

Even more startling was the realization that he would do practically anything to see her smile again.

"What are you thinking right now?" he asked.

"That you're really not at all what I expected."

"I take it that's a good thing."

"Yes. And no."

Their eyes caught and held. Hers were bright and inquisitive. With a shadow of vulnerability that he might never have noticed, had he not been looking so hard. Normally that would be enough to send him running in the opposite direction. Instead he was that much more intrigued. Everything about her fascinated him.

He reached up to touch her face and was surprised when she let him. "What would you say if I asked to see you again?"

She thought about that for a second, then answered, "I think I would say, why me?"

"Why not you?"

"Because there are hundreds of other women here, any number of them more…acceptable. All clamoring for your attention. Why pick on me?"

He'd been asking himself that same question all

night, and damned if he could figure it out. "Honestly, I have no idea."

But he hoped she would give him the chance to find out.

Everything in Lizzy told her to get away, but she felt rooted to the floor. Not that she would get far with Ethan still clutching the lapel of his jacket.

She was outside in a dark, secluded corner of the balcony, no one else around, with a total stranger— a man whose reputation *far* preceded him—yet she didn't feel the least bit alarmed.

Instead she felt an undeniable curiosity to see what he would say next. What he would do. Although, she had a pretty good idea.

He stroked her cheek and she could feel herself starting to melt, her head going loopy. His eyes searched her face, as though something about it fascinated him. Then he said the words she both longed for and dreaded to hear. "Can I kiss you, Lizzy?"

God, yes, she wanted to shout. And the fact that he'd been polite enough to ask, made her want it that much more. Already her heart was beating faster, her lips tingling in anticipation.

But as much as she wanted him to, she knew it wouldn't be right.

Not only would it not be right, it would be bloody *crazy.* He was a multimilionaire prince.

"I would prefer you didn't."

"Because I'm not your type?"

Because you're wonderful, she wanted to say. *Because it would be so easy to let myself fall for you.* But she couldn't exactly tell him that, could she? So instead she said, "Something like that."

"I can see your pulse." He stroked her throat with the backs of his fingers, barely more than a tease, and her knees started to feel squishy. "Which means you must be excited."

"I'm just a little breathless from the dancing."

He grinned and shook his head. "Lizzy, you're telling another fib."

She liked the way he said her name. The playful tone he used. God help her, she *wanted* him to kiss her. Just to know what it would feel like. Would his lips feel different than the average man's? Better somehow?

Honestly, what would be the harm in *one* little kiss?

Her head was telling her that this was a really bad idea, but those frantic words of warning were being drowned out by the relentless thud of her own heartbeat.

"One kiss," she heard herself say.

"One kiss," he agreed, lowering his head as she rose up to meet him halfway. And the instant before his lips brushed hers, he added, "Or two."

But by then it was too late. He was kissing her and all she could comprehend was his mouth, and her mouth. The soft but firm pressure of his lips. The salty-sweet taste of champagne when his tongue touched hers. Then his arms were around her and she found herself pressed against the length of his body. Her breasts, her stomach, the tops of her thighs. The cool night air brushed her skin as the jacket slipped from her shoulders. She could feel the rapid-fire pounding of his heart keeping perfect time with her own.

She knew she should stop him, but her body, her thought process, had switched to autopilot. And all she cared about, all she wanted, was to be closer.

She'd done some reckless, ill-advised things in her twenty-nine years, but of them all, nothing this bad had ever felt so good.

He broke the kiss, pressed his forehead to hers and said in breathless whisper, "I have a room in the palace."

She knew without explanation that he wasn't giving her a geography lesson. And God help her, she would have said yes. She would have said yes to practically anything just then. But the instant she opened her mouth to say the words, she heard the distinct sound of someone clearing their throat. Then a voice, calm and controlled—but undeniably firm—said, *"Ethan."*

A voice all too familiar.

Lizzy froze with terror and Ethan cursed under his breath. He let go of her slowly, taking his time, before turning to face his half brother. The king. And Lizzy did the only thing she could—curtsied and lowered her eyes to the floor, hoping like hell he didn't figure out who she was.

Talk about a mood killer.

"Yes, Your *Highness?*" Ethan said, his tone balancing precariously on the thin line between firm and sarcastic.

"It's time for the unveiling. Your presence is required in the parlor."

The unveiling of the current family portrait. Lizzy had almost forgotten. She both cursed and thanked God for his very lousy timing.

"I'll be right there," Ethan said.

The king looked from Ethan to Lizzy, and as she glanced up through the fringe of her lashes, she could swear she saw a hint of recognition in his eyes. But it was fleeting. With any luck he would focus only on the fact that he'd caught the prince and some unidentified woman groping like two hormonally challenged adolescents. She was sure that to him, women like her were a regular routine and not worth his time or energy.

"See that you are," he finally said, then turned and walked back inside.

Lizzy breathed a quiet sigh of relief.

Ethan turned to her. "I'm sorry."

She shrugged. "It's okay."

"No. It was rude of me not to introduce you."

Is that why he was apologizing? If he only knew how completely fine it was that he hadn't. So much for the kiss being harmless.

"Well, then," she said, "I guess you have to go."

"I guess." But he didn't sound very happy about it. He leaned down and retrieved his jacket from the floor. He offered it back to her but she shook her head. So he slipped it on. "Tell me you'll stay awhile."

Now she couldn't stay. If she did, and someone

recognized her, and it got back to the king and queen, it would be all over. She had to leave. "I can't. I've stayed too long already."

"What's wrong? Will you turn into a pumpkin at midnight?"

She smiled. "Something like that."

"I have to go out of town tomorrow, but I'll be back later in the week. Can I see you again?"

Oh, how she wanted to say yes. But not only was her job at stake, she was sure that next week there would probably already be someone new and he would have forgotten about her anyway. Why put herself through that? The waiting. The wondering if he would call. It was best to end this right here, right now. "I don't think that would be a good idea."

He looked more amused than insulted by her snub. "Because I'm not your type?"

Considering what they had just done, that flimsy excuse wasn't going to work again. "Because it's just not a good idea. I had a nice time tonight, though."

He looked as though he wanted to argue, then changed his mind. "How will you get home?"

The same way she got here. "A cab."

"Let my driver take you."

Did she want to ride home in a cab or the luxury of a shiny, new Rolls-Royce?

"Please," he said. "It's the least I can do."

Something deep down told her that she shouldn't, but he had said please. And, what the heck, she could think of it as her final hurrah.

"All right," she agreed, and could see that he was pleased.

"I'll arrange it with my driver and he'll meet you out front."

"Thank you."

He turned to leave, then hesitated. "Maybe I'll see you again someday?"

"Maybe." But even if he did, he probably wouldn't know it was her. He would walk right past her with barely a glance, because to him she would be nothing but an employee. A nobody.

The thought made her both sad and relieved.

He flashed her one last adorable, sexy grin, then he was gone. And she couldn't help thinking that he knew something she didn't.

Three

"Did you go?" Maddie demanded, her call waking Lizzy from a dead sleep bright and early at eight the next morning.

She sat up and rubbed the sleep from her eyes, her first coherent thought of Ethan. "I went."

Maddie squealed with delight. "Was it as marvelous as you'd hoped?"

Beyond marvelous. "I guess."

"You *guess?*"

Maddie was her best friend. Confidants since the first day of primary school. They told each other everything. But for some reason, Lizzy couldn't bring herself to tell her about Ethan. The dancing and the kissing. Maybe she was worried that Maddie would hear in her voice, silly as they were, the feelings she had for Ethan. Feelings she was sure would be as fleeting and insignificant as the time they'd shared.

This was a secret Lizzy felt compelled to keep. "I wasn't there long."

"And I was stuck in the kitchen until the wee hours," Maddie said with an indignant snort. "We must have made a million hors d'oeuvres. Boy, can those people eat."

Having worked in the palace even longer than Lizzy, Maddie had developed a certain degree of contempt for the royal family, and the wealthy jet set in general. Lizzy worried, should Maddie let her feelings slip in front of the wrong people, it might get her into trouble one of these days.

"*Those* people pay your salary," Lizzy reminded her, not for the first time. Being stuck in the kitchen all the time, Maddie didn't have much exposure to the family. Lizzy had always been regarded with respect, and since the queen's arrival from America last fall, she had never been treated so kindly, or fairly. But no matter how many times she tried to convince Maddie, she still harbored this irrational animosity.

Maddie would have been ecstatic at the idea of Lizzy kissing the prince, infiltrating their turf.

In hindsight, it was a stupid, irresponsible thing to do. And Lizzy swore she would never put herself in that sort of dangerous situation again.

"Why didn't you stay?" Maddie asked.

"I just felt out of place."

"Well then, I guess I owe you dinner and a pint," Maddie said, then went on to talk about something that happened in the kitchen during the party, but Lizzy was only half listening.

What if someone *had* recognized her? The king had looked at her, but had she really seen recognition or mere curiosity? And if the king did recognize her, the whole kingdom would know of her late-night affair with the prince.

Lizzy spent the rest of the week trying to forget about Ethan and that wonderfully, fantastically, amazing kiss. She convinced herself that if he had known who she was, he never would have so much as talked to her. She was an outsider. Not a beggar by any means, but she was staff, far enough below his class of people to not merit a second glance. Royals did not intermingle with commoners.

So even if she had agreed to see him again, the instant he realized she worked for the queen, it would have been *hasta la vista*, baby.

That was what she had been telling herself, anyway. It helped that Ethan had been away on business all week. Or so she had overheard from the queen. By Friday evening when she left for home to get ready for that dinner and a pint Maddie owed her, she was over it. In fact, she had developed something of a renewed outlook on her love life.

Since her divorce, when it came to romance, she was convinced that part of her had died. Spending that short time with Ethan, feeling those feelings again, made her realize that maybe there was life after divorce. Maybe she could find love again.

She took a little extra care getting ready, seeing that her makeup and hair were just right. She even dressed a bit sexier than usual, thinking that maybe, just maybe, a man would catch her eye.

The doorbell rang just as she was digging through the closet for her heeled boots. She glanced at the digital clock by the bedside table and saw that Maddie was ten minutes early.

She abandoned her search and jogged through the living room in her stockinged feet to the door. She unlatched the dead bolt and pulled the door open, ready to congratulate Maddie for not being late for a change, the words dying in her throat, and her good mood fizzing, when she saw that it wasn't Maddie standing there.

"Hey, love," her ex-husband said, wearing that smarmy smile she detested.

She was so not in the mood for this. "What do you want, Roger?"

His eyes traveled up and down her body in a way that made her feel violated and unclean. "Baby, you look smashing."

She shifted so that she was partially behind the door. "If it's money you need, that well has dried up." She'd learned her lesson the first two times she'd loaned him money that, to date, he had yet to pay back. Probably because he never held down a job long enough. He was an artist. A long time ago she used to find that sexy. Before she realized he used the title as license to be a bum.

"Baby, you know I wouldn't do that."

Yes he would, but she was in no mood to argue. "Then what do you want?"

"You know that several of my pieces were on display at the gallery on Third Street?"

She shrugged impatiently. Like she even cared.

He pulled a wad of cash from the inside pocket of his jacket. "I sold two."

"Smashing. You can pay me what you owe me." She could use a bit of extra spending money. By the time she put money in savings, paid the bills, then sent some to her mum in England, there wasn't a whole lot left for splurging.

"That's why I'm here," he said.

She reached for the cash, but he snatched it from her grasp.

"Let me take you to dinner. To celebrate."

Not in this lifetime. The mere thought filled her with disgust. Not that Roger was physically repugnant. Quite the opposite. He was a blond Adonis, with a dazzling smile and a sharp wit. And she was sure the other women he had been with during the course of their marriage would agree.

"I have plans," she told him.

"A date?"

"That's none of your business. Are you going to give me the money or not?"

"That means you're going out with Maddie. Dinner and a pint, is it?"

She held out her hand. "The money."

"Only if you go to dinner with me."

"Absolutely not."

He shrugged and tucked the money back into his pocket. "No dinner, no money."

"Fine." She didn't have time for his twisted little games. "*Goodbye,* Roger."

"Lizzy," she heard him say, taking far too much satisfaction from slamming the door in his arrogant face. And knowing he would be bold enough to walk in uninvited, she snapped the dead bolt in place.

As she was heading back to her bedroom, the phone rang. It was Maddie.

"I'm leaving now. I'll be there in ten. Twenty if there's traffic."

Which would make her late, as usual. "I'll see you then."

"Oh, and it's raining, so bring a jacket."

"Call me when you get here and I'll run down." No point in both of them getting rained on. She hung up the phone and was about to resume her boot search when the bell chimed again.

Did Roger not understand the meaning of the words *absolutely not?* She ignored it, hoping he would go away, but after a minute or so, he knocked.

"Bloody hell!" She stomped to the door, tired to death of his games. She unsnapped the bolt and yanked it open. "I told you that I will not—" But it wasn't Roger at her door this time. And she was so stunned to see him, she had to blink several times to make sure her eyes weren't playing tricks on her. Then he grinned, and she knew it couldn't be an illusion.

She was so stunned, she completely forgot to curtsy. Or address him by his proper title. "Ethan?"

He leaned against the door frame, dressed in slacks and a black leather jacket dotted with rain. His hair lay in soft, loose waves around his face, and he wore that adorable sexy, teasing grin. The one she hadn't been able to get out of her head for the better part of a week.

"Not who you were expecting?" he asked.

She shook her head. "What are you doing here?"

"I told you that I wanted to see you again. So here I am."

"How did you—" Before she could complete the sentence, she knew. Bloody hell, how could she be so stupid? "Your driver. That's why you offered the ride. So you could find out where I live."

He only grinned, but she knew she was right. She should have known when he'd offered her a ride that something was up.

Who knows, maybe deep down she had known. Maybe she had unconsciously hoped he would find her. And now that he had, every emotion she'd felt for him, the desire and soul-deep longing to be close, all came back to her in a heady, molten rush.

"Can I come in?" he asked.

"I'm going out." Then she added for good measure, "On a date."

"Just for a minute."

Maybe she should. Maybe she should come clean with him. She could claim that she'd been intoxicated—which wasn't a complete lie—and that was the only reason she hadn't been honest about who she was. They could go their separate ways and with any luck he wouldn't have her fired because she kept her identity from him.

She stepped back and motioned him inside. "Only for a minute."

He stepped inside and she shut the door behind him. His presence was overwhelming in the small room, as though he was eating up all the breathable oxygen. And as a result, she instantly began to feel light-headed.

"As you can see, it's not exactly the palace," she said.

He gazed around her cozy apartment, that up until that instant never seemed inferior to her. Now it seemed small and insignificant.

"It's great," he said.

Obviously he was missing the point. "Ethan, why are you here?"

Tell him where you work. And for whom.

He slipped out of his jacket and draped it across the back of her couch. Underneath he wore an emerald-green cashmere sweater that fit him just right. "You could offer me a drink."

"Your brother—"

"*Half* brother."

"Your *half* brother, the *king*, wouldn't approve. Trust me."

He sat and made himself comfortable on her couch. "Is that why you were so secretive at the party? Did you think it would matter?"

"It *does* matter. As a member of the royal family—"

"Let's leave my family out of this, okay? Just tell me, was I imagining things, or did we connect the other night?"

"Ethan—"

"Did we connect? Or are you going to try that *you're-not-my-type* excuse again."

He was completely missing the point. And she couldn't help but suspect that he was missing it on purpose.

She took a deep breath and blew it out. "Yes, we connected."

He sat up, elbows resting on his knees. "Do you like me?"

"What?"

"You heard me. Do you like me?"

Bugger, he was direct. *Tell him who you are, and put an end to this immediately.* But she couldn't make herself say the words. Instead she said, "Your minute is up."

He rose to his feet. "Do you, Lizzy?"

There he went again, saying her name, making her go all soft and mushy inside. *Just tell him already.* "You should leave."

"Do you like me?" He walked toward her, stealing all of her precious air again. "A simple yes or no."

She retreated a step, then another, then her back collided with the door. And he was right in front of her. Blocking her way, smelling so wonderful she was practically drunk from it.

She never should have let him in.

He had to know she was toast. Now he was just toying with her. To see how long it would take to completely break her will.

Probably not long.

And what was it that she was supposed to tell him? There was something…

He flattened his palms on the door, one on either side of her, boxing her in. His mouth this close to hers, the heat of his body seeping through the weave of his sweater to smother her skin.

"There it goes again." He touched that same spot on her throat as he had the other night, stroking lightly with the backs of his fingers. "I guess it's not from the dancing this time, huh?"

Her heart was pounding like mad and her knees were absolutely useless. Why didn't he just get on with it and kiss her already?

He drew the tip of one finger across her lower lip and she was wound so tight, she actually shivered and her breath caught in her throat.

He leaned in, his mouth close to her ear, and said softly, "I think you like me, Lizzy, even if you won't admit it. And that's good, because I like you, too."

Then he nipped her earlobe with his teeth, just hard enough to startle but not to cause pain. And though she tried to stop it, a sound forced its way up from deep inside her, something resembling a moan, but more…desperate.

Why did he have to be so bloody direct? So… honest? Her first mistake was letting him in. No, her first mistake had been agreeing to dance with him. She was already on mistake three or four tonight. Maybe even more.

She held her arms at her sides, hands balled into tight fists, to stop herself from doing something monumentally stupid. But she suspected that it was already too late. She could feel herself caving. And just as she decided to give in, to wrap her arms around his neck and kiss him, the bloody phone started to ring.

It rang once, then twice, then she heard a car horn out front.

Maddie was here to pick her up. Bloody hell.

Lizzy couldn't decide if her timing was good or lousy. Or maybe a bit of both.

"Let me guess," he said, a flicker of amusement in his eyes. "Would that be your date?"

She nodded.

"Nice guy. He can't even come to the door?"

"It's my friend Maddie," she admitted. "We're supposed to go out for dinner and a pint."

"So, you lied to me."

Well, duh! "Of course I lied. I was trying to get rid of you!"

The phone went silent for several seconds, then started ringing again, and there was another beep from out front. This one longer and more impatient.

"I should get that," she said, slipping out from under his arm and dashing to the cordless on the table by the couch. "Hey, Maddie."

"Aren't you ready? Let's go before all the tables are full up."

She glanced over her shoulder at Ethan, where he leaned casually against the door, watching her. She couldn't think straight when those smoky eyes were fixed her way, so she looked at the window instead, into the rainy darkness.

"Lizzy? Are you there?"

This was it. She could leave now and put an end to this. For tonight anyway, and possibly forever. Or she could stay. With Ethan. Knowing exactly what that would mean.

This time, it wouldn't end with a kiss.

Four

"Maddie, something came up and I can't go out tonight," Lizzy told her. Ethan knew as well as she did what that meant. She could feel it. The air in the room seemed to shift, become just a little thicker. A bit harder to pull into her lungs.

"What happened?" Maddie asked, sounding alarmed. "Are you okay?"

"I'm fine." Lizzy could hear Ethan's steps against the hardwood floor as he walked to where she stood. She could feel his presence behind her. "A…friend stopped by."

"Don't tell me Roger is there."

"No, it's definitely not Roger."

Maddie absorbed that, then asked, "Is this a male friend?"

One of Ethan's hands folded over her shoulder, large and steady. "Uh, huh."

"An attractive, *available* male friend?"

His other hand settled on her hip and she shivered. "More or less."

"Which part. Attractive or available?"

His hand slid around to her stomach and he eased her back against him, pressed the long, solid length of his body to hers. And, oh, did it feel good. And it was apparent, from the ridge beneath his slacks, that he was enjoying this just as much as she was. Though she doubted it was the novelty for him that it was for her.

How long had it been since a man had touched her this way? Since she'd let one. Or, God, how long since she'd *wanted* one to? Pressed up against Ethan, absorbing his warmth, surrounded by his scent, she felt so...*alive*. As if she'd been asleep and was just now waking up and feeling things again.

She closed her eyes and let her head fall back against his wide chest. She could hear his heart beating, feel the thu-thump against her cheek as she leaned into him.

"Lizzy, are you there?" Maddie asked.

She'd almost forgotten about the phone still pressed to her ear. "Maddie, I'm going to have to call you back."

"You better," Maddie said. "And I'm going to want details."

She felt Ethan's breath on her neck, felt the hand

on her stomach slide up. Over her rib cage, around her breast…

"Bye Maddie." She pressed the disconnect button and tossed the phone onto the couch, then turned so she was facing Ethan. His lids looked heavy, his eyes shiny. "Commit this to memory, because it isn't going to happen again."

She could swear she saw disappointment flicker in his eyes, but it was gone so fast, she was sure it had been an illusion.

"I guess I'll just have to work extra hard to make it memorable," he said, then he picked her up— actually swept her off of her feet. She'd read about men doing that in books, but she didn't think it actually happened in real life. At least, not to her.

If he really was trying to make it memorable, it was working.

He carried her into her bedroom and set her down on her feet beside the bed. She took quick inventory of the dimly lit room. Clean sheets on the bed, no discarded undies on the floor. Not perfect, but presentable enough for a one-night stand.

Then he kissed her and she stopped caring about the room and started thinking about the fastest way to get him out of his clothes. It had been a long time since she'd been with a man, and now that she was so close to making that leap, she couldn't seem to get there fast enough. She had the feeling that, since the moment he'd pulled her into his arms on that dance floor, this had been inevitable.

She shoved at his sweater and he helped by tugging it up over his head. She touched him, put her hands on his chest. His skin felt hot to the touch, the muscle solid underneath. She ran her hands across his shoulders, down his biceps.

This wasn't like her. This total lack of inhibition. Not that she had ever been shy when it came to sex, but she barely knew him, nor would she ever get to know him. Maybe that in itself was reason enough to let her defenses down. Since there wouldn't be a second chance.

He tugged at the buttons on her shirt, but he was taking too long. "Tear it off."

It was his lack of hesitation that was so arousing, the swift jerking motion that had her buttons flying in all directions and landing with sharp little snaps on the hardwood floor, the rush of cool air against her hot skin. He popped the snap on her bra and the instant her breasts were exposed, he took one in his mouth. It felt so good her legs nearly gave out.

This man who was touching her intimately was wealthy beyond her wildest dreams. Not to mention a *prince*. So why did she not feel the least bit intimidated? How was it that two people so completely different could be perfectly in sync?

But then he hesitated. He cradled her face in his hands, looked her in the eye. "You're sure about this?"

She had never been so sure of anything in her life. And the idea that he cared enough to ask made her want him that much more.

"I'm sure," she said, then she wrapped her arms around his neck, pressed the length of her body against his and kissed him. After that, everything was something of a blur. A frenzied contest to see who could undress the other faster. They tore at each other's clothes, and he was so beautiful, so *perfect*.

They fell into bed naked, rolled and tumbled, the struggle for the upperhand becoming more fevered. She ran her nails along his body, and nipped him with her teeth, and the more aggressive she became, the more it seemed to turn him on. And she *liked* it. She'd spent years being proper—the proper employee, the proper wife—and she couldn't stand it another second. Just this once she wanted to feel wild and out of control. Just this one time, then she would go back to being the Lizzy everyone expected.

She let down her guard for just a second and Ethan rolled her onto her back, pinning her wrists to the mattress. But rather than feel intimidated, or trapped, she was even more excited. She wrapped her legs around his waist, arched against the long, hard length of him, milking the deep groan that pushed out from his lungs. Then he pulled back and bit out a curse.

"What's wrong?"

"I just realized, I don't have a condom."

"What?" He had to be kidding. "How can you not have a condom?"

"I didn't come here with the intention of sleeping with you."

She couldn't come this far, only to have it fall apart. She was so hot, she was half tempted to tell him to do it anyway, but that was how disasters happened. Things like diseases and unwanted pregnancies. Not that she thought for a second that he carried a STD. But the fear of getting pregnant was enough to keep her mouth shut. Then she remembered, there used to be a box in the nightstand drawer. "Check the night-stand drawer. There may be some in there."

He let go of her wrist so he could lean over, and in his haste, yanked the drawer so hard it came dislodged and crashed to the floor, its contents spilling everywhere.

"Sorry," he said.

She didn't give a damn about her furniture. "Are they there?"

He leaned over, squishing her with his weight for a second. "Aha!"

He triumphantly held up the box.

"Thank God!" She grabbed it from him and dumped the contents out on the mattress, snatched one up and ripped it open.

He tried to take it from her, and she said, "Let me."

He watched with heavy lids as she took him in her hand and very carefully, very slowly, rolled it on.

"Keep that up and you're going to set me off," he warned, and she had half a mind to do just that, but the second the condom was on, he manacled her wrists in his hands and pinned them again.

"Are you ready for me, Lizzy?"

"Yes."

He rocked his hips, sliding the length of his erection against her. The sensation was so erotic, she gasped and arched against him. "You sure?"

She answered him though gritted teeth. "Yes."

He did it again, but slower. One excruciating inch at a time. "Tell me what you want, Lizzy."

One more and he was going to set *her* off. She tugged against his grip, but he held tighter, pinning her with his weight. She groaned with frustration, but he wouldn't give in. Wouldn't give her what she wanted. Even worse, she could see from his wicked smile that he was enjoying this.

"I'm just going to torture you until you say the words." Making good on his threat, he lowered his head and nipped the swell of her breast with his teeth. Then he took the tip in his mouth and sucked hard, hard enough to make her gasp in surprise and struggle uselessly beneath him.

"Tell me," he coaxed. And because she couldn't stand it another second without going completely out of her mind, she told him, in very direct and graphic language, exactly what she wanted him to do.

He plunged inside her, so swift and deep it stole her breath. He stayed that way for several heartbeats, nestled deep inside of her, then he eased back, inch by excruciating inch. He held himself there, very still, his eyes pinned on hers, for several long seconds, then rocked into her with a force that made her cry out.

"Too much?" he asked, his voice gravely, eyes glazed.

"No," she answered, but it didn't even sound like her voice, and her vision was fuzzy, as though she was watching the scene unfold through a fogged camera lens. "Do it again."

He eased back, then plunged forward. Again. And again. And then she stopped counting. Stopped thinking about anything but how good it felt. The way their bodies moved together, hips thrust in perfect sync. She knew without a doubt that she would remember this moment for the rest of her life. The instant she found perfection. Figures she would find it with a man she could never be with. But that didn't even matter now. All she cared about was this moment. Their release came simultaneously, deep and intense, and the force of it seemed to suck every last molecule of energy from her and all she could do was lay there, limp and useless.

"You still with me?" she heard Ethan ask, but he sounded far away.

She pried her eyes open to look up at him. He was propped up on one elbow grinning down at her.

She took a long, deep breath, then blew it out. "God, did I need that."

"You say that like we're finished."

That had always been the drill with Roger. One time and he was out for the count. And only if she was lucky would she be satisfied, too. "We're not?"

His smile grew and he got this adorable, devilish gleam in his eye. "Sweetheart, I'm only getting started."

Hours later Lizzy lay draped across Ethan, their arms and legs tangled, her head resting on his chest, more sexually satisfied than she'd felt in her entire life. The man was unstoppable. If she did an Internet search on the word "stamina," Ethan's photo would pop up on the screen.

The bed was in shambles, the comforter shoved down and bunched up at the footboard and the top sheet twisted. The bottom sheet had pulled loose and was coming off one corner. Add to that the clothes strewn on the floor and the contents of her drawer spilled and it looked as though a hurricane had ripped through her bedroom.

They may have been all wrong for each other, but there was no denying they had the sexual compatibility thing to a science. Unfortunately that was all they had. And sex just wasn't enough for any kind of lasting relationship. Not that she was looking for that, and she knew for a fact that Ethan wasn't a settling-down kind of man.

As it was, though, she was in danger of falling deeply in lust with him.

"You tired?" Ethan asked, shifting against her. He slid a hand down her back and with the other started to play with her breast.

She looked up at him like he was nuts. "You have got to be kidding me."

Ethan grinned.

"You should have rolled over and gone to sleep hours ago. You're like the Energizer bunny."

"Is that what Roger does?"

"Roger?" How did he…?

"When you were on the phone you said it wasn't Roger. Is he your boyfriend?"

If she didn't know better, she might suspect that he was a little jealous. "Ex-husband. And yes, his…*performance* was less than memorable. With me anyway. I can't speak for the other women he slept with during the course of our marriage."

"Ouch."

"The first time I caught him cheating he was so miserable. He cried like a baby and begged me to forgive him. So, like a fool, I did."

"How long were you married?" he asked.

"Four years. Four years too long." She had no idea why she was telling him this. Maybe because he made her feel comfortable, she knew instinctively that he wouldn't judge her. Talking to him felt…natural. It was weird how they had breezed right past that new relationship awkwardness. Not that they had a relationship. What they did have was sex. Correction, *had*. They *had* sex—great sex—and now it was over.

She untangled herself from his limbs and sat up, covering herself with the sheet. "I have to work in the morning."

"Saturday?"

She nodded and shrugged. "Sorry."

"Sounds like you're kicking me out."

More like saving him the trouble of coming up with an excuse to leave. "I'm afraid so."

He didn't argue, didn't try to change her mind. He just sat up and started putting on his clothes. That was a good thing, so why did she feel a dash of disappointment? This was exactly what she wanted, right?

Since it was likely going to be the last time she ever saw him this way, she watched as he dressed. Bloody hell, he was beautiful. As long as she lived, she would remember this night.

He pulled on his slacks and stood to fasten them. "You know that I didn't come here to sleep with you. I just wanted a chance to get to know you."

"And you did." In the biblical sense, no less. "Now it's over."

He cast her a wounded look that was about as genuine as she was royal. "I feel so...*used*."

"I'm sure you'll recover." Not only that, but she had saved herself the necessity of trying to explain who she was and why she'd lied to him in the first place. In a week or so, he would have moved on to the next woman and wouldn't even remember her name. It probably wouldn't even take him that long.

When he was dressed, she rolled out of bed and grabbed her robe. The least she could do was see him out. They walked in silence to the door, then he turned to her.

"I had a good time tonight."

"Me, too."

"If you change your mind—"

"I won't."

"Don't be so sure. I'm pretty irresistible."

"You just keep telling yourself that."

He opened the door and leaned in the jamb. "One kiss for the road?"

She rose up on her toes and pressed a kiss to his cheek. "Goodbye, Ethan."

This was best, but as he stepped into the hall, why did she have to force herself to shut the door behind him? And why did she press her ear to the door to listen to his retreating footsteps?

To be sure that he really left. That's all. She couldn't have him loitering out in her hall. What would the neighbors think?

She locked the door and latched the chain then turned off the lights. It was when she walked back into her bedroom that she saw it lying on the floor with contents of her bedside table drawer. Ethan's watch.

She picked it up and sat on the edge of the bed. It was a Rolex, in solid platinum. It had to be worth thousands, so how could he just forget it? Or maybe he hadn't. Maybe he'd left his watch there on purpose, so she would have to see him again. Honestly, she wouldn't put it past him. He was a man who was used to getting what he wanted.

Wouldn't he be surprised when this time she wasn't so quick to succumb to his charms.

Five

Ethan met his cousin, Charles, at their health club the next morning for their weekly game of squash. And though Ethan usually slaughtered him, today he was off his game by miles.

"What's up?" Charles asked as they walked to the locker room. "You usually kick my ass all up and down the court."

"Guess it's just your lucky day." It didn't help that he'd only gotten an hour or two of sleep. Or that a certain woman had been on his mind all morning.

He opened his locker, peeled his sweaty shirt off and tossed it in.

"Jesus," he heard Charles say from behind him. "I should have known."

He turned to him. "What?"

"That it was a woman distracting you."

What was he, telepathic? "Why would you think this has anything to do with a woman?"

"I guess you haven't looked in a mirror lately."

He glanced in the mirror on the inside of his locker door, but other than appearing a bit tired, he didn't look any different than usual. He shot Charles a questioning look.

"Other side," Charles said.

Ethan turned and looked back over his shoulder, realizing instantly what Charles meant. There were scratch marks—deep ones—crisscrossed all up and down his back. That explained the sting he'd felt when he'd soaped up in the shower this morning.

Charles wore a cocky grin. "You going to try to tell me a woman didn't do that?"

"It was a woman," Ethan admitted. An amazing, spectacular woman who he hadn't been able to keep his mind off of.

"So, you got yourself some crumpet," Charles said.

"I don't even want to know what that means." Because if it was coming from Charles, it was most likely X-rated.

Charles just laughed.

Inside his locker, Ethan's phone began to ring. He looked at the display, but it was a blocked call. Something told him he should answer it. "I have to take this."

Charles grabbed a towel from his locker. "I'm going to hit the shower. I'll meet you in the bar."

"Order me my usual," Ethan said, then answered the call with a cocky, "I told you that you couldn't resist me."

There was a long pause, then Lizzy's voice, sounding suspicious. "How did you know it was me?"

Ethan laughed and admitted, "Lucky guess. Although I would love to know how you managed to get my private cell number."

"Let's just say I have connections."

"Military intelligence?"

There was a brief pause, then, "I could tell you, but then I would have to kill you."

He considered that for a second, then dismissed the possibility. She was too sweet, too feminine, to be military. The only logical explanation was that she knew someone in the royal family, or at the very least someone with connections to the royal family, and had gotten his number through them. But at this point, did it really matter?

"You left your watch here," she said.

"I know."

"So you actually *admit* it?"

"I didn't leave it on purpose, if that's what you're implying. I was halfway to my car when I realized I wasn't wearing it. I would have come back, but I had the sneaking suspicion you wouldn't let me in."

"I'm supposed to believe you didn't leave it here on purpose?"

"If I wanted to see you again, do I strike you as the kind of man who would need an excuse?"

"Honestly, could you be more arrogant?"

And could she be more brutally honest? But that was one of the things he liked most about her. She was tough. With a soft, gooey center. "I could be there around seven."

There was another pause, then, "Make it eight."

"Eight it is, then."

"Be forewarned that I'm not letting you inside. I'm not even going to unlatch the chain. I have no intention of sleeping with you again."

And he had no intention of leaving her apartment until he'd seduced her. But he didn't tell her that. "That's fine. I just want my watch."

"Fine. I'll see you at eight," she said, then the line went dead.

He grinned and tossed his phone back in his locker. She seemed pretty intent on keeping the upper hand, but what she didn't realize is that she was already as good as his.

When Lizzy looked up and saw the queen standing in her doorway, she snapped her cell phone shut. How long had she been standing there? And how much had she heard?

"I'm sorry," the queen said. Well into her eighth month of pregnancy, her rounded belly proceeded her into the room, and her gait had taken on a slight waddle. "I didn't mean to interrupt."

Lizzy wanted to ask how long she had been standing there, but she could never be so rude. She stuck her phone in the top drawer of her desk. "No, ma'am, I'm sorry. I should never have accepted a personal call at work. It was totally inappropriate of me."

"Elizabeth, it's Saturday for heaven's sake. You should be at home. I though we agreed that you would take some time off to relax."

An entire day sitting at home alone, with all the time in the world to think about Ethan? She would rather be at work. "I had a few things to do that couldn't wait."

The queen sighed and shook her head. "You're hopeless."

She had no idea how right she was about that. How pathetic was it that Lizzy had so little a life, she preferred to spend her Saturdays in the office? "Can I get you something?"

She shook her head. "Backache. I've found it helps if I walk around."

Lizzy could only imagine what it would feel like to have a little human being growing inside her. She used to think that she would have children. She'd always wanted to. Now she wasn't sure if that was in the cards for her. She didn't want to be a single mother, and since her disastrous first marriage, she had vowed never to tie the knot again.

The queen gave a little gasp and flattened a hand on her belly. "He's kicking, want to feel?"

Lizzy nodded eagerly. Because she knew the queen loved to share her experiences, and also because it made Lizzy feel a little less like a subordinate.

The queen walked around her desk, took Lizzy's hand and placed it on her belly. A second later she felt a very pronounced thump against her palm.

"The kicks are so much stronger now."

The queen smiled. "Sometimes I think he's trying to beat his way through my belly. I've enjoyed being pregnant, but I think I'll be glad when it's over." She put her hand over Lizzy's and gave it a squeeze. "You've been such a wonderful help these past few months. I probably don't thank you often enough."

Her words filled Lizzy with guilt. The truth is, the queen thanked her constantly. And how did Lizzy repay her? By going behind her back and breaking the cardinal rule of her employment. At least she would never find out. Even if Lizzy had to live with the guilt for the rest of her life.

"Well, I should let you get back to work. Don't stay too late."

Lizzy dropped her hand from her belly. "I won't, ma'am."

She half walked, half waddled to the door, then paused before stepping into the hall. "You know, Elizabeth, men do so enjoy a good chase. But don't play too hard to get."

So she *had* heard her conversation. Lizzy's cheeks blushed with embarrassment and she scrambled for something to say, but before she could, the queen was gone.

That was too close. If the queen had figured out

who Lizzy had been talking to, it would have been a disaster. But how could she?

Inside her drawer, she could hear her phone vibrate. She opened it and checked the screen. It was Maddie. And it was at least the tenth time she'd called. Lizzy could only put her off for so long.

At the risk of being caught in a personal call again, she pulled her phone from the drawer and answered it, "I'm at work."

"I know," Maddie said apologetically, "but the suspense is killing me! How did it go last night?"

She kept her voice low, in case one of the office girls was in the vicinity. "It was…enlightening."

Maddie squealed with delight. "Are you saying you actually put an end to over a year of abstinence?"

"Hard to believe, I know."

"No, that's fantastic! Who is he? Someone I know? Are you going to see him again? Tell me everything! I want details!"

Unfortunately she couldn't give her any. Considering Maddie's opinion of the royal family, she would very likely interpret Lizzy's actions as some sort of mutiny. Besides, it would be best if no one knew what she had done. "It was one night, now it's over."

"What? *Why?*" Maddie sucked in a breath and asked, "Bloody hell, did he dump you?"

Lizzy could feel her bristling through the phone line, and couldn't help but laugh. Maddie was always there, watching her back. If it hadn't been for her,

Lizzy might never have survived her divorce. "No, nothing like that. I told him I only wanted one night."

"He was that lousy?"

Lizzy laughed. "No, he was fantastic. I'm just not in the right place for a relationship."

"Who is he?"

"Just a guy. Someone very bad for me."

"Another artist?" she said with an indignant snort.

"Something like that."

"Well, I'm sorry it didn't work out, but I'm so glad you finally took the plunge, so to speak."

So was she. And tonight was it. The last time she could ever see Ethan again. She would give him his watch, then close the door on him for the last time.

When Ethan walked into the bar Charles was at their usual table near the fireplace, just below the widescreen HD television, flirting with a young, attractive waitress. Women found him charming, and his looks irresistible. He was the kind of man that other men looked at and thought, Damn I wish I looked like him.

He was with a different woman every week, and sometimes several at once. Dating was like a sport to him. And though he never led any woman to believe he would be exclusive, they all seemed to think that they would be the one to change him. And they tried. But Ethan couldn't imagine him ever settling down.

The waitress walked away and Charles followed her with his eyes.

Ethan crossed the bar and took a seat at the table, where his drink waited for him. "Cute waitress."

Charles nodded, not peeling his gaze from her shapely behind.

"She doesn't look familiar."

"She started Wednesday. Great body, don't you think?"

"Ask her out yet?"

She disappeared through the door leading to the kitchen, and Charles finally turned to look at him, grinning from ear to ear. "We're meeting for drinks tonight."

Ethan laughed and shook his head. "You don't waste any time."

He shrugged. "Don't see the point in waiting. No time like the present, right?" He took a swallow of his drink. "So, tell me about this woman. Anyone I know?"

"I don't think so. I met her at the gala."

"The woman in the gold dress?"

Ethan nodded. "You know her?"

"I remember thinking that she looked familiar. I was going to ask her to dance, but you beat me to it. Who is she? Who's her family?"

Ethan shrugged. "No one. She's a secretary. Lives in a small apartment in town."

He narrowed his eyes. "Is it serious?"

"It was just sex, and one night," he said, and when Charles raised one questioning brow, he added, "Her rules, not mine."

"Sounds like my kind of woman."

That's exactly what Ethan thought. At first. But Lizzy had gotten under his skin. "I want more."

"More sex?"

"More…something." He shrugged. "I like her, Charles."

"I don't have to tell you how that's going to go over with your brother."

"Half brother," Ethan automatically corrected. Despite their blood ties, there was nothing familial about their relationship. Phillip never missed an opportunity to remind him of his illegitimacy. Even if it was nothing more than a scathing look. Ethan always knew his place. "And since when do I give a damn what Phillip thinks."

"Maybe you should. You're in a sensitive spot with the partnership."

"If he pulled anything now, Sophie would eviscerate him."

"He's not afraid of Sophie." Maybe not afraid, but Sophie had more influence over her brother than Phillip would ever admit. On tenacity alone, Sophie always seemed to get what she wanted. "You know that Phillip is stubborn enough to make your life hell," Charles warned.

Charles would know. He and Phillip had been close friends since childhood. And though Ethan trusted Charles to a certain degree, because of his ties to the king, theirs was a complicated relationship. Ethan made it a point to be very careful what he said to him. Especially when it came to the partnership, as, among other things, Charles acted as attorney for the royal family. But like Sophie, and despite the tension it might have caused, Charles welcomed Ethan into the family and treated him as an equal. And for that Ethan was grateful.

"Speaking of business," Charles said. "I've been gathering information on the Houghton hotel, like you asked."

The Houghtons owned a hotel that had been in their family for generations, and just happened to sit adjacent to the building the royal family was renovating, not to mention on the prime resort land on the island. "Do you think they'll sell?"

"If not, we can acquire it at auction in a few months. Old man Houghton has gotten himself into something of a financial jam. He's so far behind in his taxes, the property will be seized, if the mortgage company doesn't foreclose first."

"So, it's as good as ours?" he asked, and Charles nodded. "What course of action do you recommend?"

"I think we should buy him out. Make him an offer he can't resist. And I think we should do it soon. If it goes to auction, someone could try to outbid us and we could pay even more than it's currently worth."

"Sounds good. Work up a proposal and we'll present it to the board."

"I'm already on it."

With business out of the way, Charles went on to talk about the "tasty little thing" he'd had the pleasure of acquainting himself with last night, and that got Ethan thinking about Lizzy. And how he would manage to insinuate himself into her apartment. Not that she'd been all that difficult to sweet talk.

He always got what he wanted.

Six

Lizzy was prepared when Ethan rang the bell that evening. She would hand him his watch, then say goodbye and shut the door, and if he knocked again, there was no way in hell she would answer it. She'd abandoned the idea of keeping the chain latched. After all, she wasn't so weak that she couldn't see him face to face without completely losing her cool.

But after a full day of anticipating his arrival, when she reached for the knob her heart leaped up into her throat.

He stood in the hallway looking delicious dressed head to toe in black. Delicious and dangerous. Appropriately so, considering what would happen if he learned who she really was. And she was so close to getting him out of her life forever.

"You look like a cat burglar," she said.

He grinned and leaned in the doorway. "Yeah, but you love it."

God help her, she did. *Give him the bloody watch and get rid of him.*

"Here you go," she said, holding it out, and he took it.

"You're not going to invite me in?"

"I thought we covered this on the phone."

He grinned and her legs felt a little wobbly. "I figured you were forgetting that you find me completely irresistible."

She folded her arms under her breasts. "My, don't we have a high opinion of ourselves."

He shrugged. "I just call it like I see it."

She was about to close the door on him forever when she heard footsteps on the stairs. She peered around Ethan, down the hall, and nearly had a coronary when she saw Roger round the corner. He was looking down at something he held in his hands. Money, she realized. He was counting it.

Damn, damn, damn! There was no way she could let him see Ethan. He would recognize him instantly and he knew the palace rules. She didn't doubt for a second that out of spite he would make trouble for her.

So she did the only thing she could. She grabbed Ethan by the front of his leather jacket and yanked him inside, slamming the door behind him.

When he got over the initial surprise of being manhandled, he shot her a smug grin and said, "You're not letting me in, huh?"

"Shh!" Barely ten seconds passed before there was a loud knock. "Don't say a word," she whispered to Ethan, and when he opened his mouth to speak, she pointed a stern finger his way. "I mean it. Shush."

She latched the chain and opened the door a crack. "What do you want?"

"Hey, love, you've got company?"

"No."

"Really? I could swear I just saw someone walk into your apartment."

"You must have been mistaken."

He shrugged and flashed her that smarmy smile. How could she have ever found that charming? "Well then, how about that dinner I promised you?"

"I already ate."

He produced the wad of money he'd been counting on the way up, as though it were some sort of bait. "A drink, then?"

"Honestly, I would rather remove my own skin with a cheese grater."

Behind her, Ethan chuckled quietly, and she swung blindly, connecting with what felt like his biceps.

Roger, on the other hand, wasn't amused. Something bitter and nasty flashed across his face. It was a side he rarely let show. "Same old repressed Lizzy," he said in a voice filled with pity. "No wonder you're still alone. And probably always will be."

No matter how many times she vowed not to let his words bother her, it still stung. He knew exactly where to strike to do the most damage. Maybe she had been a little cold during the last year of their marriage. Call her crazy, but after a spouse cheats, it pretty much dooms the concept of intimacy. Every time he touched her, she pictured him with someone else.

The truth was, she'd stayed with Roger after that first time, but she'd never really managed to forgive him. And maybe if she had, maybe if she had let him back into her heart, he would have been faithful.

There you go, Lizzy, blaming yourself again.

"Last chance," he said, waving the money under her nose like bait.

She wasn't that hard up for the cash he owed her. "Keep the money and just consider us even," she said, then took extreme pleasure from slamming the door in his smug face. She leaned her forehead against it, closed her eyes and sighed.

"Let me guess," Ethan said. "Roger?"

She nodded.

"Nice guy."

"Charming to a fault," she agreed.

"And for the record, you're the least repressed woman I've ever met in my life."

Did he have to be so darned nice? Why couldn't he be the arrogant, womanizing jerk she had heard so many things about?

"You know what this means, don't you?" she asked.

"What?"

She turned to face him, leaning her back against the door. "Just to prove him wrong, I'm going to have to sleep with you again."

"Revenge sex?"

"You've got a problem with that?"

He shook his head. "Just as long as you realize that you've got nothing to prove. I know how passionate you are."

It wasn't Ethan she needed to prove it to. Hell, maybe she didn't need to prove anything to anyone. Maybe she just needed an excuse to sleep with him one more time and this was as good a one as any. At this point, did it even matter why?

She would sleep with him one last time. One more night together—the entire night this time—and she would never see Ethan again.

Ethan walked Lizzy backward toward her bedroom, kissing and undressing her along the way. He flung her shirt onto the floor and unsnapped her bra with the ease of a man who had removed a bra or two in his time. He hadn't seemed to notice that she wasn't exactly voluptuous. Or maybe he did, and just didn't care. Not every man liked large breasts.

More than once Roger had not so subtly suggested she consider implants. He had excelled at finding every one of her physical imperfections. And a few others that, she realized later after she'd kicked his sorry ass out, didn't even exist.

This is not the time to be thinking about Roger, she reminded herself.

Besides, Ethan seemed perfectly content with her breasts and more concerned now with getting her jeans unbuttoned and pushed down her legs. She helped, then kicked them off and out of the way.

He slipped a hand between her legs, stroking her through her panties, lightly though, so it was more of a tease than an actual touch. And so erotic she shuddered.

"Lay down," he ordered, and she did, anticipation making her shiver. He knelt on the bed, between her legs, still fully dressed. He hooked his fingers in the waistband of her panties, eased them down and slipped them off. She was naked, and he was staring at her, his eyes black with desire. "You're amazing."

She tried to think of some snappy comeback, but her hormone-drenched brain was incapable of all but the most basic functions.

Ethan put his hands on her thighs, easing them apart. She knew instinctively, by his body language and the expression on his face, what was coming next. At least, she *hoped* she did.

Ethan lowered his head, and when she felt his mouth brush her inner thigh the sensation was so erotic she nearly vaulted off the bed.

He looked up at her. "Good or bad?"

"Good," she said, but the word came out as more of a croak.

"Are you sure?" He made a move like he might back away. "I can stop."

"No!" That time it came out loud and clear, and Ethan grinned.

He touched her inner thigh, starting at the knee, and slowly stroked his way upward. He lowered his head and took her in his mouth, and the feeling was so deeply rooted, so explosively physical, she could barely stand it. She turned her head into the pillow to muffle a moan of pleasure.

It had been so long, *too long*, since anyone had touched her this way, and she wanted it to last, but she could already feel herself unraveling. She curled her fingers into the sheets, digging her heels into the mattress as every muscle in her body coiled tight, then peaked and let go in a hot rush. Wave after wave of pleasure washed over her and she slowly sank back down, feeling limp and sated.

"You still with me?" Ethan asked.

She opened her eyes, saw that he was kneeling over her. Her eyes drifted upward, until she reached his face, a satisfied grin curling the corners of her mouth. "Oh, yeah."

He grinned. "You all right?"

"Hmm. That was…" She sighed, unable to put into words exactly how she was feeling. Maybe there were no words to describe it. So she settled for a simple, "Wow."

* * *

It was official.

Ethan had just had what was by far the best sex of his life. He and Lizzy lay side by side in her bed, naked, sweaty and breathless, and too spent to move a muscle. He could barely work up the energy to breathe.

"What time is it?" she asked.

"Why, are you going to kick me out again? Let me guess, you work Sundays, too."

"I'm not kicking you out. I can't see the clock, and I was curious as to how long we've been at it."

He craned his neck to see the digital clock on the bedside table. "It's eleven-forty."

"Three and a half hours? Wow."

And he could be expecting fresh scrapes on his back. If they kept this up, he was going to make her either cut her nails or wear gloves. But according to her, they wouldn't be doing this again. "Can I ask you a question?"

"Sure," she said.

"Why do you let what he said bother you?"

She exhaled a long sigh. "It's complicated."

"Is that code for it's none of my business?"

There was a pause, then she said, "The second time I caught Roger cheating, he said it was my own fault. I was so cold that I drove him to it."

"You're not cold."

"Maybe I was then. It's hard to be intimate with someone when you know they've been unfaithful."

"That isn't your fault."

"Maybe not, but he knows it bothers me, so when he's angry it's the first thing he pulls from his bag of tricks." She rolled over onto her stomach and propped herself up on her elbows. Her hair tumbled across her shoulders and down her back. He reached out to touch it, curling a lock around his finger.

"Have you ever been married?" she asked.

"Nope."

"Ever come close?"

"Never."

"Is it marriage in general that you're against?"

He shrugged. "Not really. I guess I just haven't met anyone I could imagine spending the rest of my life with."

"But if you did?"

He turned to look at her. "Why, are you interested in the position?"

"God no!" she said a bit too forcefully, then added, "No offense."

"None taken."

"Really, it has nothing to do with you personally. I won't ever get married again. To *anyone*. When I was with Roger I felt so…out of control."

"You like being in control."

She nodded. "I'll be the first to admit that I'm a control freak. It took me a long time to get back to feeling as though I was my own person again. I'm still not one hundred percent there."

"Well, for the record, I'm in no rush to tie the knot. I enjoy my freedom."

They were both silent for a minute, then she said, "Can I ask *you* a question?"

"Sure."

"When did you find out who you are? Or did you always know?"

"Are we talking self-awareness or genetics?"

"Genetics."

His parentage wasn't something he was ashamed of, but he also didn't feel the need to talk about it. In fact, he preferred not to. He preferred to keep his private life private. But for some reason, talking to Lizzy didn't bother him so much. Maybe because she was so damned honest with him. "I was in college."

"Your mom told you?"

"She died before she got the chance. Honestly, I'm not sure if she ever would have." And he would always wonder why. If she had done it to protect him, or to protect herself. "She told me my father was a businessman who traveled a lot and didn't have time for us."

"You grew up in the U.S.?"

"In New York. We moved there when I was a baby. But she was born here, in Morgan Isle."

"She died young?"

"Very young. She was only thirty-nine."

"Was she sick?"

"Car wreck. I was going through her things afterward and found financial documents. Apparently they had an agreement. As long as she kept her mouth shut, there would be monthly checks until I reached the age of eighteen. If she ever told anyone the truth, the funds would stop."

"I guess I can see why the king wouldn't want it to get out. They don't like scandal."

"She didn't have an agreement with the king. It was Phillip's mother, the former queen."

Her mouth fell open in surprise. "The *queen* paid her off?"

He nodded. "To be honest, I still don't know if my father even knew about me. I probably never will know. After the queen died, Sophie learned the truth, pretty much the same way I did, and contacted me. She talked me into visiting."

"If she hadn't, do you think you would have ever connected with the royal family?"

"Probably not." He rolled onto his side to face her. "But I'm glad I have Sophie in my life."

"And the king."

"We *tolerate* each other." Barely. But they were brothers—if only half—and more or less stuck with each other. And he didn't want to talk about this any longer. It was too...depressing.

He reached out and touched her hair, brushing a pale lock back from her face and draping it over her shoulder. "Let me take you out."

"Right now?"

"Tonight, tomorrow. Whenever."

She looked away. "I can't."

She puzzled him. It seemed as though every time he made a connection, she cut him off at the pass. In his experience it was usually the woman grasping for connective tissue. Lizzy was different than any woman he'd ever been with. "Sure you can. You don't want a commitment, I don't want a commitment. It's perfect."

"It wouldn't work."

He stroked his hand down her back, over the swell of her behind, and she made a purring sound deep in her throat. "If you ask me, everything works just fine."

She shot him a look. "You know what I mean. We're too different."

Most women went after him for his money. This is the first time he'd met one that was intimidated by it.

"Lizzy, I'm not asking for your hand in marriage. Just dinner. Besides, I've dated *my kind*. Maybe I'm looking for something different."

"Maybe I'm not."

"How will you know unless you give it a chance?"

She groaned and dropped her head in the pillow, then offered him a muffled, "Has anyone ever told you that you're unbelievably stubborn?"

He grinned. "All my life. And I usually get what I want." He gave her a nudge. "One date. That's all I'm asking."

She looked over at him, her eyes filled with regret. "I can't. I wish things were different. I really do. Can't we just enjoy this night together and leave it at that?"

And she called him stubborn? But this wasn't over. "If that's what you want."

"It really is."

He wasn't kidding when he said he always got

what he wanted. And he wanted her. And though it might take time, he would wear her down.

Eventually she would see things his way.

Seven

Lizzy came awake slowly, the scent of something delicious tickling her nose. Bacon, she realized. And freshly brewed coffee. For a moment she was sure it was the fringe of some wonderful dream, but when she opened her eyes, it didn't disappear. Then she heard the sound of dishes clanking together from the open doorway.

Either someone had broken into her apartment or Ethan was making her breakfast.

She had to remind herself that he wasn't always a wealthy prince. He was a self-made millionaire, rejected by the man who'd fathered him. Only recently had he connected with the royal family.

But that didn't change who he was. Someone who could potentially get her fired.

She sat up and looked at the clock. It was after nine. She never slept this late. Even on a Sunday. But that was bound to happen when one spent three-quarters of the night having sex.

To say it had been fun was the understatement of her life, but now it had to end.

She crawled out of bed and slipped into her robe. She used the bathroom then fastened her hair up into a ponytail and brushed her teeth. There was a wet towel hanging on the rack, meaning he must have showered. It was a wonder that she'd slept through it.

She found Ethan in the kitchen, his back to her, dressed in his slacks and shirt, the sleeves rolled to the elbows. His hair was wet and slicked back from his face and he was barefoot. She watched him from the doorway. She didn't know why, but there was something so intimate about a barefoot, recently showered, sexy man in her kitchen making breakfast.

She gave herself the luxury of one brief, warm fuzzy feeling, then steeled her emotions and reminded herself that this was the first and last time she would be seeing him this way.

He startled her by saying, without even turning around, "Good morning. There's fresh coffee."

"How did you know I was standing here?"

He turned to her. His shirt was unbuttoned, showing off his perfectly toned chest. Forget breakfast. He looked good enough to eat.

"I can feel you thinking," he said. "Working out how you're going to get rid of me."

Was he psychic or something? "Really?"

"Honestly? No. I saw your reflection in the microwave. I just guessed about the other part. I was right, though, wasn't I?"

She figured it was best not to answer that. "You're up early," she said instead, though it was late for her.

"I don't sleep much."

She stepped closer, the scents from the stove making her mouth water. "What are you making?"

"Eggs and bacon. I hope you don't mind that I made myself at home."

Even if she did, it was a bit late to do anything about it. Besides, it was kind of nice not waking to a quiet, empty apartment. Not that she would ever admit it to him. Or even wanted to make a habit out of it. She liked being alone, living by her own schedule. Setting her own rules.

Eating when she wanted to eat, sleeping when it suited her. Sole possession of the remote control. These things were precious.

She took a seat at the table. "I never imagined you as the cooking type."

"I am more than just a pretty face. In fact, there's a lot you don't know about me." He opened the cupboard to the left of the sink and pulled two mugs out. "How do you take your coffee?"

"Cream and sugar." It was a bit unsettling, how

quickly he had acquainted himself with her kitchen. How easily he had insinuated himself into her life.

This is what she got for not booting him out last night.

He fixed her coffee and set it on the table in front of her, then went back to the stove.

She sipped, then asked, "So, why does a gazillionaire prince need to learn to cook?"

"I didn't always have money." He used tongs to flip the bacon frying in one of the pans. "Besides, I like cooking."

"How did you wind up a hotel mogul?"

"I worked my way through college in the hotel business. I started out as a bellboy."

"Seriously?" She couldn't see him hauling luggage. Royals didn't even carry their own luggage, much less someone else's.

"I started at the bottom."

"How do you go from bellboy to owner?"

"Hard work." He turned to her and grinned. "And a rich partner."

A partner who was even richer now, since he'd embezzled and dropped off the radar. But she didn't mention that. He would wonder where she'd gotten her information, and she might have to admit that it came directly from the royal family. Information was the one advantage to being invisible. People said things in her presence that they wouldn't normally admit.

"You have me at a disadvantage," he said. "You

know quite a bit about me, but I know next to nothing about you."

And she intended to keep it that way.

She got up and walked over to the window, the hum of traffic on the street below rumbling through the panes. It was dark and dreary and spitting rain. "Not much to tell."

"You've lived here all your life?"

"I grew up in England, actually. My mom and two sisters still live there. I moved here to go to university on a scholarship."

"Are you the oldest? Youngest?"

"What difference does it make?" She turned to face him, to tell him he had to go now, and nearly collided with his chest. He was right behind her, and she hadn't even heard him cross the room. "What are you? Part cat?"

He grinned and tugged her to him by the tie of her robe. In the process, the bow came loose and her robe fell open.

He made a sound of appreciation in his throat, kind of a sexy growl. "You're naked under there."

She reached for the two sides, to yank them closed, but it was too late. His hands were already on her, touching her. And when he touched her, she lost the ability to think logically.

He lowered his head and nibbled her neck and a shiver coursed through her. "I hope you didn't have plans today."

If she had, she couldn't remember them now. Not

with his lips on her neck, his hot breath on her skin. His big, warm hands cupping her breasts.

She tried a futile, "You need to leave." But they both knew where this was going, and his leaving was no part of it. He was already walking her in the direction of the bedroom. Kissing her. Touching her.

"The food," she reminded him, but he was feasting on her skin instead, and his glassy-eyed, heavy-lidded look told her he was too far gone to think of anything else.

"Honestly," he said, flashing her that hungry grin, the one that made her go weak in the knees. "I think I'd rather have you for breakfast."

Honestly, that sounded pretty good to her, too. So she didn't put up a fight. But as soon as they'd had their *breakfast,* he was out of there.

Ethan didn't leave her apartment until after the sun set that evening. And when he told her he had to travel to the U.S. on business Monday morning, and wouldn't be back until the following Friday, it had been a relief. With any luck, he would meet someone else and she would never hear from him again.

At least, that's what she was telling herself. Until the first batch of flowers came Monday evening. A mixed bouquet. An explosion of color wrapped up in a bow. Wild and beautiful, yet delicate somehow. And there was a handwritten card that read, *These reminded me of you.* It wasn't signed, but she knew who had sent it.

A second bouquet, larger and more colorful than the last followed on Tuesday. The card on that one said simply, *Missing you*. Another came on Wednesday, and a fourth on Thursday. At which point her apartment was so stuffed with fresh flowers it was beginning to smell like a nursery.

By Friday, she sat on pins and needles, missing him terribly and anxious to see him again. She even left work a bit early to primp. She sat eagerly, watching the time tick by on the clock, waiting for that inevitable knock on her door. She turned on the television and switched through the cable channels, stopping on a film about a group of women on a road trip that looked entertaining, but it only barely held her attention.

By ten she began to suspect that he wasn't going to show. By eleven, the hollow pang of disappointment filled her stomach. At midnight she switched off the television and crawled into bed.

Something must have happened between the time he'd bought Thursday's flowers and the time he'd left the plane. She should have been relieved that it was over, instead she felt like the world's biggest fool.

She had fallen for him. Hard. She a lowly secretary in deep lust with the Prince of Morgan Isle. At least now she wouldn't have to figure out a way to explain who she really was.

On Saturday, she sat at her desk sulking most of the day, not getting much done. Trying to tell herself that it was for the best. Wallowing in self-pity.

Honestly, what had she expected? That he would sweep her off her feet and make her a princess? She didn't even *want* that. The life of a royal was so cloying and suffocating. To be under constant scrutiny from millions of people, to regularly see her own name in the papers and tabloids. She couldn't imagine anything worse. She would much rather be invisible.

Around noon, when the queen called Lizzy to her suite, she had herself thoroughly convinced it was for the best. If she never saw Ethan again, that would be a good thing.

Lizzy knocked on the door of the queen's suite and she called her inside. She stepped in and shut the door behind her. The queen was in her favorite chair with her feet up, and there was a man sitting on the sofa. It took several long seconds to register that it was Ethan. And when it did, she froze. Every instinct told her to turn around and dash back out the door. Or to take the leather binder she held and use it to cover her face, but she was too stunned to move a muscle. To even blink her eyes.

She'd heard the reference "a deer in headlights" and realized this was how the poor deer probably felt.

Ethan glanced up at her, briefly, fleetingly, then looked away, dismissing her as just another random employee. And she held her breath, hoping, *praying,* it didn't register. Then his gaze snapped back in her direction and recognition filed his eyes.

Oh, *bloody hell.*

She knew this was bound to happen. Knew it the instant he asked her to dance at the gala and she didn't tell him the truth right then. It had just been a matter of time.

"Elizabeth, what does my schedule look like on June eighteenth?" the queen asked, and for one tense, excruciating moment, Lizzy just stood there, unable to respond. Unable to move a muscle. And Ethan just stared, but she could see his mind working, see him figuring things out.

And he wasn't happy.

"Elizabeth?" the queen asked, looking concerned. "Are you all right?"

Lizzy could only imagine how her face must have looked. She pulled herself together and forced a smile. "Yes, sorry. What was it you wanted to know?"

"My schedule on the eighteenth of June. The prince has asked me to come and tour the progress on the hotel." She paused, looking back and forth between them, then asked, "Have you two met?"

At first she thought the queen had caught on to their discomfort, then realized she was only being her usual polite self.

"No, ma'am, we haven't," Lizzy said, praying that Ethan went along with it, that he wouldn't put her on the chopping block.

"Ethan," the queen said, "this is my assistant, Elizabeth Pryce."

She performed the formal curtsy, even though she knew Ethan hated that. It wasn't as if she had a choice. He was royalty. Technically, that is. When he was naked in her bed, their bodies entwined, his hands on her skin, then he was just Ethan.

But she had the feeling that he would never be *just Ethan* again.

Ethan smiled warmly and addressed her with a nod and a polite, "Miss Pryce."

"Or is it 'Mrs.'?" he asked, though he knew darned well she was divorced. Not that she could blame him for his skepticism. She should have told him who she was. The instant he approached her at the gala she should have been honest.

But then she would have missed out on those two wonderful days with him. And she wouldn't trade those for anything. He'd made her feel alive again, like a whole person, and for that she would always be grateful.

"Miss," she said, and because she couldn't bear to look at him another second, knowing what must be going through his head, the betrayal he must feel, she busied herself with opening the leather binder and checking the queen's calendar. "You have a morning meeting with the chairman of the Hausworth Children's Foundation, but you're free that afternoon."

"Perfect!" the queen said. "Could you please pen in a visit to the hotel?"

"Of course, ma'am."

The queen turned to Ethan. "Shall we say one o'clock?"

"Perfect," he agreed, then rose to his feet. "I should be going. I appreciate the advice."

He couldn't be more pleasant, but she could hear a tone in his voice, see a glimmer of something dark and unpleasant in his eyes. Underneath the good cheer, he was fuming.

And she couldn't blame him for it.

The queen smiled, blissfully unaware there was a problem. "I'm happy to help. Anytime."

He walked toward the door, his eyes on Lizzy, and she stepped out of his way, probably a bit too far, so he could pass. And she couldn't help but wonder what advice the queen had given him.

"It was a pleasure to meet you, Miss Pryce," he said. His voice was courteous, but his eyes belied his anger.

She curtsied again. "Your Highness."

Then he left and shut the door behind him, and Lizzy took her first full breath since she'd stepped into the room and seen him sitting there.

"He's very sweet," the queen said, then added, "And handsome."

Lizzy nodded and uttered a noncommittal, "Hmm."

"You don't think so?"

What was she getting at? Did she suspect something? She didn't want the queen to think she found Ethan attractive, but if Lizzy played it too casual, would she be even more suspicious?

She settled for a non-answer. "He looks very much like the king."

"Yes, he does. And they have the same stubborn

streak." She sighed and waved away the thought as if it were a pesky insect. "Oh, well, I'm sure they'll come around and start seeing each other as family."

Somehow Lizzy doubted that. "Is there anything else, ma'am?"

"No, Elizabeth, you can go. I'll call if I need you."

She curtsied, then opened the door and stepped out into the hall. The instant it was shut and she was alone, the gravity of the situation hit her hard. She leaned against the door, weak-kneed and trembling.

She had brought this on herself. She could only hope that Ethan took pity on her and didn't report what she'd done to the royal family. But honestly, she wouldn't blame him if he fed her to the wolves.

Eight

Lizzy walked back to the administrative wing where her office was located, thankful that she didn't run into anyone along the way. Since it was Saturday, only a few secretaries were working, but for the most part the entire wing was deserted.

She stepped into her office, walked to her desk and set down the leather binder. She'd been clutching it so firmly her fingers ached. In fact, she was so tense, she ached all over.

Behind her the door snapped closed and she spun around in surprise.

Ethan stood there glaring at her. "You're just a secretary, huh? Miss *Sinclaire*."

Whatever emotion he'd been hiding back in the

queen's suite, he let go now with a force that nearly knocked her physically backward. He wasn't just angry or hurt, or even disappointed. He was livid.

"Sinclaire was my married name. I wanted to tell you the truth. I *should* have told you."

"You think?"

"I'm sorry."

"Did you plan this all along," he stormed. "Did you think you could seduce your way into the family?"

Plan it? Was he kidding? Did he really have the gall to suggest that *she* had seduced *him?* "That's completely unfair," she snapped back at him, keeping her voice low so no one else would hear. "Maybe I wasn't totally honest with you, but you know bloody well that you were the one to seek me out. You asked me to dance at the gala, and you were the one to show up at my apartment."

"And at no point you felt it necessary to tell me who you really were?"

"If I told you who I was, and you got angry, sort of like you are now, I could lose my job."

"So, what you're saying is, you didn't trust me."

"I didn't *know* you. I wasn't even supposed to see you again."

"You could have told me at the gala, when we were out on the dance floor."

She lowered her eyes. "I know, and I should have, but I was…curious."

"Curious?"

She looked up at him. "Okay, sue me, but just for

one night I wanted to know how the other half lived. I wanted to feel like I belonged. I know that's a horrible offense, for a commoner to step above her station. I figured, what the hell, it's just one night. But then you kept coming back."

"You lied to me."

She couldn't deny it. She'd never actually said she *didn't* work for the palace. But lying by omission wasn't any less deceitful. "You're right. I made a mistake. And I'm sorry. If I could go back and do things differently, I would."

He just stood there, staring, his eyes boring through her like lasers. It was worse than any words he could have flung at her.

"Are you going to tell the queen?" she asked.

"Are you asking if I'm going to get you fired? Do you really think I would do that?"

She bit her lip, ashamed for even suggesting it.

"And here I thought you were different. I thought you actually saw me." He shook his head, disgusted, and even worse, disappointed. "I guess I was wrong."

"I don't know why it even matters. It was over. You got back from your trip yesterday, yet I didn't see you."

"My flight was delayed. I got back this morning." He narrowed his eyes at her. "Were you waiting for me last night?"

Why did she have to go and open her big mouth? "Of course not," she said.

He wasn't buying it. "Another lie, Lizzy?"

Did he want to completely strip her of her dignity?

Would that make him feel better? Well, fine, he could have it. "Yes, I waited for you. I wanted to see you. Even though I knew we had no future, no hope of this relationship going anywhere. Our social differences aside, I tried the marriage thing once before and I don't ever want to put myself through that again. And no offense to you personally, but I find the life of a royal suffocating and claustrophobic. I wouldn't wish it on my worst enemy."

She couldn't tell if he was insulted or disappointed or just plain angry. His face gave nothing away.

"We had good sex, Ethan."

"Great sex," he corrected. "And that's all it was ever going to be."

"And now it's over." Because as much as she cared for him, lusted after him, they had reached a dead end. There was nowhere left to go.

"Well, then," he said, his hand on the doorknob, "I guess I'll see you around."

"Maybe." But she hoped not. "And by the way, thank you for the flowers."

He paused for a moment, as though he might say something, and she realized there were so many things she wanted to say to him. Mostly she wanted to thank him. For reminding her what it was like to feel passionate and alive. That there was more to life than work and responsibility. For making her feel…happy. But she couldn't make herself say the words.

And by the time she worked up the nerve, he was already gone.

* * *

Lizzy had only been home a few minutes when her phone rang, and her heart jumped up into her throat. Then slid right back down again when she looked at the caller ID and saw that it was Maddie and not Ethan.

"A couple of us are meeting at the pub tonight," she told Lizzy. "Want to come with?"

The only thing she wanted to do was to change into her pajamas, curl up on the couch and feel sorry for herself. "I don't think so."

"Oh, come on. I've hardly seen you for weeks. And I still owe you dinner and a pint."

"I'm not feeling very good," she said, and it wasn't a lie really. She felt lousy. Heartsick and guilty. And sad. Deep-down-into-her-soul sad. And not so much because it was over, since it was bound to end eventually anyway, but because she was pretty sure that not only had she made him angry, but she'd hurt him, as well.

"I hope you didn't work today," Maddie said. "If the queen finds out you're sick and she in her fragile state catches it, they'll sack you for sure."

Sometimes Lizzy got so tired of her backhanded comments about the royal family. What had they ever done to Maddie, other than supply her with reliable employment for the past twelve years? But she bit her tongue. She had given up trying to convince Maddie that the new queen was nothing like the former. Nor was Phillip like his father. In fact, he seemed to go out of his way lately to distance himself from that distinction.

"Maybe we can go out next weekend," she said instead.

"You know what we need? A girl's weekend away. Maybe we could catch a bus and spend a few days on the other side of the island. We could shop until we drop, drink ourselves silly and meet sexy, un-available men. What do you think?"

Meeting more men was the last thing Lizzy had on her mind right now. "I really can't leave. Not with the queen so close to her due date."

"Why?"

"She might need me. What if she goes into labor early?"

"So what? It's not like you're delivering the baby."

"But I want to be there."

"*Why?* I mean, honestly, Lizzy. Why do you even care? Do you think they give a damn about you? Well, I hate to break it to you, but they don't. You're just a servant to them. A glorified slave."

Lizzy bit her tongue so hard she tasted blood. Maddie would never understand. She wouldn't even try. "I'm going to let you go, Maddie."

She sighed, probably thinking that Lizzy was hopeless. A lost cause. "Take care of yourself. Eat chicken soup. I hope you feel better soon."

"Thanks. I will."

"I'll call tomorrow to check on you."

"Bye." She hung up and set the phone back in the

cradle. Then she turned and looked around the apartment. It was the same as it had been before Ethan showed up at her door that first time, but for some reason it felt different. Empty and far too quiet. Maybe she should have taken Maddie up on her offer. Maybe she should have gone out and had fun and forgotten about Ethan.

But she had the sneaking suspicion that he was going to be hard to forget.

After leaving the palace, Ethan had gotten into his car and driven. To no place in particular. Through town, then up the coast. He drove for hours, trying to clear his head, replaying what Lizzy had said. At first he was so angry, he was sure that he would stay mad at her forever.

When she'd walked into the queen's sitting room, he hadn't recognized her right away. He'd never imagined her looking so plain and unassuming. She bore no resemblance to the feisty, passionate woman he had come to know. It was as if she were two completely different people.

And maybe she had lied to him, but she was right about one thing. He had been the one to pursue her. Accusing her of using him had been a cheap shot, and said out of anger. He'd made the first move at the gala, and he was the one to keep coming back. How many times had she said it had to end, but he hadn't listened?

And he still wasn't listening. Because he was accustomed to getting what he wanted. And despite everything that had happened, her deceit and their angry words, he wanted *her.* And why did their affair have to end? Neither wanted a relationship. It was the ideal arrangement. Now he could have his cake and eat it, too.

He got out of his car and walked to the building. He let himself inside and climbed the stairs to the second floor. The hallway was empty and quiet. From outside Lizzy's door he could hear the low hum of the television playing.

Only for an instant did he question if he was doing the right thing, then he raised his hand and knocked. A moment later he heard the unlatching of the chain, the turning of the dead bolt, then the opening of the door.

Lizzy stood there, dressed in her robe, even though it was only nine o'clock, looking exhausted. But not all that surprised to see him. Only then did he realize how much he had missed her in the week he'd been gone. And how much he didn't want this to end.

"I wondered if you were ever coming up," she said. When he regarded her questioningly, she added, "There aren't too many people in this neighborhood who drive expensive black sports cars. Back to berate me again?"

"I just want to talk."

She hesitated, then stepped back and gestured him inside. The room was dim but for the light of the television. She walked over to the end table and switched on a lamp. "What do you want to talk about?"

"Us."

"I thought we already established that there is no us."

"I want you to know that I realize the position I put you in by pursuing you, and I understand why you weren't completely honest with me. Why you handled things the way you did. And I was overly harsh. I should have been more understanding."

"You had every right to be angry."

"Would you stop that?" he snapped, and she flinched. "Stop blaming yourself. I acted like a jerk and I'm trying to tell you I'm sorry."

She bit her lip and lowered her head, and for an instant he thought she might cry. But when she looked up again, her eyes were dry. She looked relieved and conflicted.

"Can you forgive me?"

She nodded. "Can you forgive me for lying?"

"I already have." He took a step toward her. "I missed you while I was gone."

She took a step back, narrowing her eyes at him. "Don't do it."

"Do what?"

"You know exactly what I mean. Don't you dare touch me. Don't even think about it."

"Why?" he asked in the most innocent voice he could manage, though he knew damned well why. When he touched her, she lost the ability to think rationally, to tell him no. Which was exactly what he was counting on.

She held up a hand, as though that would be enough to stop him. "Just keep your distance."

"Did you miss me?"

She just stared at him.

"Lizzy?"

"Of course I did! But that doesn't make our relationship any less doomed. This will never work."

"On the contrary, I think it's perfect. Neither of us wants a commitment, and you can't say the sex isn't fantastic. I mean, honestly, what more could we possibly ask for? It's the perfect situation. We get to indulge without the strings."

"There's one thing that you're forgetting. I still work at the palace, and you're still a prince."

"What I do in my personal life is no one else's business."

"This isn't just about you. I happen to enjoy being employed. I can't throw away a career I've spent years building for a night in bed."

"No one has to know."

"So, what, we're going to sneak around? Hope no one recognizes us? You're a prince, for God's sake. People know who you are."

He took another step toward her and this time she stood her ground. She was trying to be brave, to be strong, but she was no match for the attraction they felt for each other. It grew and pulsed around them, like a living, breathing thing. "You can't deny that you want this as much as I do."

"Wanting something doesn't mean it's good for you," she said, but he could see the conflict in her eyes. She was so close to cracking. All he had to do was to touch her and she would melt.

He moved closer. "Admit it, Lizzy. Tell me you want me."

Her throat worked as she swallowed. "You know I do. But that doesn't change anything. This still isn't going to work."

He reached out and curled a hand around her waist, tugged her closer to him. So she would be forced to meet him halfway. And she didn't fight it. She went willingly, melting against him, pressing her cheek to his chest.

"This is a mistake," she said as she wrapped her arms around him, inside his jacket, her body warm and soft, squeezing as though she never wanted to let go. She breathed in deeply and exhaled hot breath against his shirt. It soaked through to his skin, warming him all over.

He stroked her hair back and tucked his fingers under her chin, lifting her face so she would look him in the eye. "Tell me, Lizzy."

She gazed up at him with sleepy eyes, her cheeks rosy with arousal. Her pulse pounding a frantic rhythm through the veins in her throat. "I want you, Ethan."

Before she had the opportunity to change her mind, he lowered his head and kissed her. She tasted warm and sweet and familiar. She wrapped her arms around his neck, pressed herself against him, as though she couldn't get close enough. It was almost eerie how perfect it felt, the depth of his affection for her. The undeniable and intense connection, as though some invisible grip kept them emotionally linked.

He could tell himself a million times that it was only sex, but he knew it was more than that. He also knew that these feelings, as intense as they might be, were only temporary.

He'd been passionate about women in the past, but it never lasted very long. A month maybe, three or four at most. He would begin to make excuses, reasons he couldn't see her. They would begin to drift, spending less and less time together. Then he would meet someone else, someone he found too fascinating to ignore, and he would end it with Lizzy for good.

That was his MO, after all. Have his fun, then get out of Dodge.

Nine

Ethan had showed up at her door Saturday night at nine, and didn't leave again until late Sunday night. And most of that time they spent in bed, crawling out only occasionally to seek nourishment to rebuild their strength. Monday, when she got home from work, he was already there, parked in the street outside her building, waiting for her. And when they stepped inside the foyer, where no one could see, he pulled her to him and planted a toe-curling, knee-weakening kiss on her.

She smiled up at him, feeling all warm and fuzzy. It was nice to have someone to come home to. Someone to share the events of her day with.

Ethan made her feel special, and it was a welcome

change. Roger certainly never had. To boost his own ego, he had always focused on her faults. And even knowing that, recognizing the behavior, it still tore down her self-esteem. And she'd stuck around too long. Maybe because she believed no one else would want her. He had *made* her believe that.

This thing with Ethan was temporary, yet he managed to make her feel more loved and accepted than Roger ever had. And she couldn't help wondering how long they would last. How long would it take for them to tire of each other? A month? Maybe two. Or would it be longer? There was no reason to put a limit on it. At least, not yet.

For the first time in her life she was going to live in the present and not worry about the future.

"If you haven't had dinner yet, I can cook for us," she said as they walked upstairs, his arm looped around her waist, hand curled around her hip. And it felt right. It was…comfortable.

He shot her a simmering smile. "There's only one thing I'm hungry for right now."

And his appetite seemed insatiable. They stepped into her apartment and she barely had time to close the door before he began ravaging her. He slipped the pins from her hair and watched it tumble down over her shoulders, then started undoing the buttons on her suit jacket.

She decided dinner would have to wait, and dragged him by the lapels of his jacket to the bedroom, where they all but tore at each other's clothes, then tossed and tumbled for the next hour and a half. Afterward, since it was late to start cooking, they ordered delivery Thai from a restaurant around the corner and ate in, talking about each other's day. It was a nice change, being able to talk about her work, not having to appease him with half truths and non-answers.

"You really love what you do," Ethan said, and since she was in midchew, she nodded. "That's good. Too many people hate their jobs."

She swallowed and wiped the corners of her mouth with a napkin. "It's been especially rewarding since the queen arrived. She's been wonderful to me. Never once disrespectful or unkind. And working in the palace for as long as I have, I've run into my share of unkind people."

"I like Hannah," he said, draining his wineglass. "But for the life of me I don't know what she sees in Phillip. They seem very happy though."

"Their marriage seemed a bit rocky at first. He wasn't around much. I could tell she was unhappy, even though she tried to hide it. I'm not exactly sure what happened, but a month or so before she announced she was pregnant, everything seemed to change. Now the two are practically inseparable. Sometimes the king will look at her and his eyes are so filled with love. It makes me think, if anyone ever looked at me that way, I would be the happiest, luckiest woman alive."

He grabbed the wine bottle from the bedside table

and emptied it into their glasses. "Except, you don't want a commitment."

She nodded. "Yes, that would be a problem. But maybe, if someone loved me that much, I would have to make an exception."

"As long as he wasn't a royal," he said with a grin. "Because that would be too suffocating and claustrophobic."

She returned his smile. "Exactly."

"Have you ever been in love like that?"

"I thought I was, with Roger, but looking back, I can see that I was just fooling myself. I wanted it so badly, to be loved and accepted, I convinced myself the relationship was something that it wasn't." She took a sip of her wine. "How about you? Have you ever been in love?"

He leaned back on his elbows. "Yep. Madly in love."

Was that a twinge of jealousy she just felt? Of course not, because that would just be ridiculous. People didn't get jealous in casual relationships. There was no point. "Who was she?"

"Allison Williams. I met her in school."

"High school or college?"

"Kindergarten," he said with a grin. "She moved away halfway through the year. I was devastated."

She laughed. "Cute. And since Allison?"

He shook his head. "No one."

For some reason that surprised her. He was so… passionate. "Why not?"

He shrugged. "No time. I have a business to

maintain and no woman can get in the way of that. I prefer a no-strings-attached lifestyle."

She set her plate on the floor beside the bed, set her glass down, then scooted close to Ethan and snuggled up beside him.

He wrapped an arm around her and pulled her close, kissed the top of her head. "I guess we don't have to worry then."

"About what?"

"Falling in love. Since neither of us is looking for that."

"Exactly," she agreed. And he was right, so why did the idea make her feel sad? The truth of it was, even if Ethan was that man, the one to look at her with that deep, unconditional love, she could never be the woman he needed. They were too different. They may have started out life on level ground, but now they were miles apart.

Who was she kidding? They had never been on level ground.

"Phillip would love nothing more," Ethan said. "He's pushing for me to settle down. He says it will be good for the family. As if I plan to live my life by their rules."

And they did have lots of rules. Hundreds of them. Working for the family was one thing, but she couldn't ever imagine wanting to be one of them. She was too independent.

Ethan lazily stroked her hip with one large, warm hand. "Can I ask you a question?"

"Sure."

"You knew the king? My father, I mean."

She nodded. "Somewhat."

"What was he like?"

She looked up at him. "You never met him?"

He shook his head. He looked so sad it nearly broke her heart.

She wished she could tell him that his father was a wonderful, noble man, but that would be a lie. "He was…complicated."

"Sophie told me that he was a coldhearted, over-bearing, pompous ass."

"Yeah, that sounds about right." She'd always had the feeling that Princess Sophie and her brother resented their father, but it wasn't as though they shared that kind of thing with the staff. And if they ever did, no one was talking. "And unfortunately, the queen wasn't much better. I always felt sorry for them, having a mother and father so cold."

"He cheated openly. Or so Sophie has said."

"He could be charming when he wanted to be." Lizzy had friends, other employees at the palace, who had succumbed to those charms. Even though it meant immediate dismissal afterward. No mistress ever lasted long.

Ethan narrowed his eyes at her. "How charming?"

She laughed. "Not *that* charming. I won't say that he didn't notice me at first. But I made it damned clear that I wasn't interested."

"That explains it."

"Explains what?"

"Why you dress the way you do for work. Why you look so plain."

"Being invisible is always easier."

He sighed. "At times I wish I'd had the chance to meet him, but I get the feeling I would only be disappointed. I think my mom knew that. It's probably why she never told me. Although I can't help resenting that she kept it from me."

"I'm sure she did what she thought was best. Just like my mom, although she failed miserably."

"How's that?"

"My father left us just after my baby sister was born. I was six. My mom tried to find a replacement, a father figure for us, but she had horrible taste in men. Most of them drank, and a few hit her. When I won a scholarship to attend school in Morgan Isle, I couldn't pack fast enough. I didn't even wait until fall, when courses began. I left right after graduation."

"Do you ever go back to visit?"

She shook her head. "Too many hard feelings, and my sisters resent me for leaving them. And sadly, they haven't fared much better in love. They attract losers. Men who drain them then move on. Not that I've been all that lucky in love myself. Roger was a leach, sucking me dry of my dignity and my money. Sometimes I think the women in my family are cursed."

"Or just unlucky?"

"Maybe. I send my mom money every month, though, to help make things a bit easier."

"Even though you resent her?"

She shrugged. "She's still my mom, still family. Despite all of her faults, I love her. You would do the same for your mom if she were alive."

"You're right. I would."

She rose up on her elbow to look at him. "I think we're both too kind for our own good."

"That would explain a lot."

"Maybe that's why this thing we have feels so nice. It's selfish. And it's bad for me. I've spent my entire life playing by the rules. It's liberating to do something just because it feels good."

"I'll bet…" Ethan rolled her over onto her back and settled himself between her thighs, grinning. "I can make you feel really good."

She didn't doubt that for an instant. No man had ever made her feel as good as Ethan did. She arched up, rubbing herself against him where she was still slick and warm from the last time they made love. She felt him pulse, growing hard and long. "I think I'm going to need proof."

He leaned down, brushed his lips against hers, soft and teasing. "And what will I get in return?"

"Anything you want."

"All I want is you," he said, and with a shift of his hips sank deep inside her. And it was just so… perfect. And so wrong. It was going to have to end, and when it did, she hoped it wasn't badly.

* * *

"Elizabeth, are you all right?" the queen asked her later that week, after, for about the third time that day, Lizzy had completely blanked out and hadn't heard the queen talking to her.

They were in the queen's sitting room, she on the sofa with her feet up and Lizzy beside her, looking at baby announcements. But Lizzy was having a terrible time concentrating. It was Ethan's fault, keeping her up way past her bedtime last night. Business meetings had kept them apart Tuesday and Wednesday, so Thursday they had spent quality time together. He hadn't left her place until after one and she was paying the price this morning.

"Fine, ma'am. I apologize. I didn't sleep well last night."

"You can go home early if you like."

She was so nice, it filled Lizzy with guilt. Lizzy was slacking off because she was having a forbidden, lurid affair with the queen's brother-in-law. "I'm fine, ma'am."

The queen held up an announcement with pastel ducks and bunnies on it. "What do you think of this one? Too feminine for a boy?"

The truth was, they had looked at so many, they were all beginning to look the same. "The one with the blue blocks is still my favorite, I think."

The queen sighed. "This shouldn't be so hard."

"You want it to be perfect," Lizzy said. She imagined she would be the same way if she ever had children. She was still young enough. And maybe, if she met the right man…

But that would be a few years down the road. Or maybe not so far. It was amazing how quickly things could change. Her entire outlook on life had changed in just a few weeks. She had let down her guard and trusted a man. If someone had told her a year ago that she would be where she is today, she would have called them crazy. But now, she could honestly say she was happy.

She wondered what kind of a father Ethan would be. Not that she thought she would ever find out. Not firsthand anyway. Did he even want children? Having a family wasn't something couples discussed in a relationship that was deemed temporary. There was no point.

"Elizabeth?"

She looked over at the queen and realized she'd been talking, and once again Lizzy had completely zoned out on her. "Sorry, ma'am."

"Is it a man? The one you were talking to the other day. Is that why you're so distracted?"

Though Lizzy tried to hide it, her cheeks burned with embarrassment. The weird thing was, she wanted to tell the queen about it. She wanted to tell *someone*. But she was the last person Lizzy should be spilling her guts to. Not only would it be totally inappropriate to discuss personal matters with her employer, but it would mean certain termination. She bit her lip, unsure of what to say.

"I'm sorry," the queen said. "I'm being nosy."

"No, it's okay. I just…" She took a deep breath and blew it out. "It's complicated."

"Are you in love?"

God, no, she would never be that foolish.

"You can tell me to mind my own business," the queen said.

"No," Lizzy said. "I just…I guess I'm not really sure how I feel about him. He's too…" She shrugged.

A hopeless romantic, the queen persisted. "Too what?"

"Too…*perfect*." If it wasn't for the fact that he didn't want a relationship, that this was strictly sex, she reminded herself.

The queen just laughed. "That's the silliest thing I've ever heard. How can a man be *too* perfect?"

"I guess what I'm trying to say is, it's so right, it must be wrong." Her own words surprised her. What she and Ethan had was as *right* as good sex could be. It wasn't anything more than that. It never would be. "We're too different."

"Sometimes different works. Look at me and Phillip. We couldn't be more different. We're from different countries, came from completely different backgrounds. Yet, we're happy."

She and the king weren't so different. They both came from money, and unlike Lizzy, the queen had royal blood in her veins. And if the queen had a clue who the man in question was, she wouldn't be so supportive.

"As I said, it's complicated."

The queen just smiled. "Whether you want to admit it or not, I can see that you really care about him."

The queen was mistaking lust and infatuation for love. But Lizzy wasn't about to admit that she would rather have a brief, no-strings-attached affair than be in a committed relationship. Even if she had a choice. Not yet anyway.

"I'm sure you noticed, but when I first moved here, things with Phillip were, shall we say…bumpy."

Lizzy nodded. "I noticed. And I'm so pleased that everything worked out."

"It just takes time." She touched Lizzy's arm. "Maybe you should give this man a chance."

She could see that it was a losing argument, so she just smiled and promised she would, and that seemed to appease her. Then Lizzy changed the subject back to birth announcements.

But she had the sinking feeling that she hadn't heard the last of this.

Ten

Ethan had missed his last two games with Charles, so Saturday morning he crawled quietly from Lizzy's bed, so he wouldn't wake her, then dressed and headed to the club. Charles was already in the locker room changing when he got there.

"I wasn't sure if I was going to see you this week," Charles said. "I tried to call you at home last night, but no one answered."

"That's because I didn't go home." He hadn't been home much at all lately. Almost all of his free time he'd spent with Lizzy.

Out of fear of being spotted, she refused to go to his penthouse apartment. Or out to dinner, or the theater. She'd never even so much as ridden in his car. So they hung out at her place, but they always managed to find something to do to keep them occupied.

"Who is it this time?" Charles asked. "Anyone I know?"

He shrugged out of his jacket and hung it in his locker. "I told you about her."

"You did?" He looked puzzled for a second, then asked, "The secretary?"

He nodded.

"*Still?* I thought that was only supposed to be one night." He paused then added. "Her rules, not yours. Remember?"

"If I want something, I go after it." He was half-tempted to tell Charles who she was. Ethan knew of at least half a dozen palace staff members who Charles had dated, and was pretty sure he could trust him. But he'd promised Lizzy he wouldn't tell anyone, and he always kept his word.

"You see her often?"

"Almost every night."

His eyes went wide with alarm. "Seriously."

Ethan nodded.

"Bloody hell. You're not worried she'll get too attached?"

"I like her, Charles. She…gets me. I can be myself when I'm with her. Besides, we've agreed to keep it casual."

Charles looked wary. "Women say that all the time. To hook us in. And before you know it they're expecting a ring and a happily ever after."

"Lizzy isn't like that. She's divorced and not looking to remarry."

"I hope you're right. It's scandalous enough to marry a nonroyal, but a *divorced* nonroyal? I think that's considered a cardinal sin."

"It's never going to be an issue. I have no interest in marrying anyone."

Charles shook his head, as though he couldn't believe it, or he felt sorry for Ethan. "I hope you know what you're doing."

"I have the best of both worlds. All the fantastic sex a man could ask for, and none of the hassle."

Ethan slaughtered Charles at squash, then, after a shower and a quick drink, decided to pay a visit to the palace. To see Lizzy, of course, since she insisted working Saturday, even though Phillip and Hannah were out for the day at some charity function. Which got him thinking about what Charles had said.

It was true that he and Lizzy were spending an awful lot of time together. Even if it was only an hour or two in the evenings. He couldn't help but wonder if he was pushing his luck, if he should take a step back.

But as quickly as the idea formed, he dismissed it as paranoia. Lizzy didn't want a commitment any more than he did. They were on borrowed time, so why not take advantage of what time they did have together?

The palace was quiet with only a skeleton staff in the administrative offices. When he entered, one of the office girls rose from her seat. She was young, probably an intern still in school. She curtsied and asked, "Can I help you, sir?"

God, did he hate being addressed that way, but he turned on the charm and flashed her a flirting smile. "I sure hope so." He looked around, as though what he had to say was a secret, and lowered his voice to a whisper. "I'd like to get a gift for my brother and his wife, to celebrate the birth of their first child, but I'm pretty clueless when it comes to things like that."

The intern nodded sympathetically.

"Would there be a way to find out what they need? Maybe someone who would know and could be discreet. I'd like it to be a surprise."

"The person you want is Miss Pryce, the queen's assistant," she said in a hushed voice.

She had no idea just how right she was about that. "I don't suppose she would be in today."

"She is, actually. She could tell you exactly what they need."

"And she'll be discreet?"

"Of course, sir. Her office is just down the corridor. Third on the left."

"Perfect. Thanks." He started to walk down the hall, then turned back to her. "Let's keep this between us." He flashed her a grin. "If anyone asks, I was never here."

"Absolutely, sir." She smiled and made a motion across her lips as though she was turning a lock and throwing away the key.

He gave a quick knock on the door and heard Lizzy call, "Come in."

He opened the door and stepped inside and she looked up from her computer. If she was surprised to see him she didn't let it show. She sat primly behind her desk, glasses perched on her nose, looking very professional. Conservative blue suit, no make-up, hair pinned sternly back in a knot.

"Miss Pryce, is it?"

She regarded him coolly, as though his being here was an everyday occurrence. "Your Highness?"

"I was hoping you could help me." He closed the door behind him. Then he locked it.

That got her attention. Her eyes went wide and she rasped under her breath, "What are you doing?"

He grinned and walked toward her desk. "What do you think I'm doing?"

It took her a moment to process what he meant, then her mouth fell open with surprise. "*Here?* You can't be serious."

"I told the girl out there that I need help picking out a baby gift for my brother. She sent me to you." He walked around her desk, then he swiveled her chair so she was facing him. "Convenient, huh?"

"Are you nuts?"

"Probably." He lifted her up and deposited her on the desktop then sat in her chair. "But you love it."

She wouldn't admit it, but she didn't have to. He could see it in her face. Her rosy cheeks and shiny eyes. She was turned on.

"We could get caught," she said, but didn't stop him when he slipped her shoes off.

He grinned up at her. "I know. That's what makes it so hot."

"Ethan, no. We can't."

"You don't mean that." He eased her skirt up, past her thighs and up around her waist, and she helped him by lifting her hips. She had on thigh-high stockings underneath and he growled with appreciation. His favorite part of the day lately had been peeling those stockings from her legs, but that would have to wait until later.

"What if someone hears?" she said, but she wasn't putting up much of a resistance.

He shrugged. "Don't make any noise."

"Easy for you to say."

He touched her through her underwear and she sucked in a breath.

"Feel good?"

She bit her lip and nodded.

"How about this?" He slipped his fingers underneath, stroked her bare skin, and she trembled. He leaned forward and kissed one thigh, then the other, and she slid closer to his face, right to the edge of the desk, her eyes glossy and half-closed. She wasn't behaving like a woman who wanted him to stop. He worked his way upward, kissing and stroking, until she all but melted into a puddle. Then he stopped and pulled away and she groaned with disappointment.

"Still want me to stop?" he asked.

She didn't answer, but her expression said it all. She was burning up. And if they had more time, he might have made her say the words out loud. But having a quick romp was one thing, taking too long would look suspicious and he didn't want to put her job in danger.

His eyes glued on hers, he hooked his fingers on the waistband of her panties and dragged them down her legs.

He had barely touched her, just one sweep of his tongue, and her entire body shuddered with release. She threw her head back, sinking her fingers in his hair, and rode it out. The intensity of it left her shaky and out of breath. And it seemed to cure her of her fear of being discovered. She gazed down at him, lips damp and red, then slipped off the desk to unfasten his belt. "No noises, remember."

Ethan was in and out of Lizzy's office in under twenty minutes, with the promise that he would see her later that evening back at her place. When he left, the girl from the outer office looked up and smiled.

"Did you get what you came for?"

"Yes, I did." That, and then some. "Thanks for your help."

He made a quick stop in the public washroom, then headed downstairs, running into Sophie on his way out. Literally. She rounded the same corner at the exact same time from the opposite direction and they collided into one another. She was so willowy and light, if he hadn't grabbed hold of her arm, he might have knocked her clear over. Which wasn't to say she was a pushover. Sophie might have appeared soft and gentle, and undeniably feminine in her gauzy dresses and silk outfits, but on the inside she was tough.

"Ethan! What are you doing here!" She threw her arms around his neck and planted a firm kiss on his cheek.

"Business," he said, and hoped she didn't press for specifics.

But Sophie being Sophie, she did. "What business?"

"I came to talk to Phillip. But he and Hannah are gone for the day."

Her brow wrinkled. "He hasn't been giving you a hard time?"

"No. No more than usual." He changed the subject, hoping he could bait her away from the topic of their brother. "Has Charles told you about the Houghton hotel deal?"

"Yes!" she said excitedly. It was Sophie who had pushed for the addition of a spa and advanced fitness center, complete with state-of-the-art equipment and staff trained in all of the latest beauty and exercise trends, not to mention two Olympic-size pools, one indoor and one out. "I'm already working with the designer I told you about. And I've ordered the appliances for the kitchen."

"Top of the line, I hope."

She grinned. "Of course. I've been busy testing new recipes for the menu. Want to come over and be my guinea pig?"

"I wish I could, but I have plans tonight."

"What kind of plans? Like a date?"

"Something like that."

She had a sparkle of curiosity in her eyes. She was forever trying to set him up with her available friends. Although, unlike Phillip, she wasn't pushing him to the altar. She just wanted him to be happy. "Really? Anyone I know?"

"I don't think so."

One brow perked slightly higher than the other. "From around here?"

"She lives in town."

"Is this a first date?"

He folded his arms across his chest. "Is this twenty questions?"

"What?" She shrugged innocently. "I can't help that I have a curious nature. You're my big brother. I like to know what's going on in your life."

He sighed. "No it's not a first date, and before you ask, no, it isn't serious. Nor will it ever be."

"So, you're having an affair?"

The term *affair* made it sound cheap or immoral, and it wasn't either. But they were engaged in a temporary sexual relationship, which he supposed, by definition, *was* an affair. "I guess you could call it that."

"Is she married?"

"Of course not!"

"Engaged?"

"Not engaged, either." What kind of man did she think him to be?

She shrugged. "Just asking."

"She's single. Divorced actually."

"I would love to meet her. Maybe we can all go out?"

That was not going to happen. "She wouldn't. She's a little intimidated by the whole royal thing. She would be…uncomfortable."

The irony of that particular lie was that in all honesty, Lizzy was probably more comfortable and more accustomed to dealing with royalty than he was. Professionally, that is.

"She would be uncomfortable, or *you* would?" Sophie asked.

Now she was fishing, and he had things to do before Lizzy got out of work. "I have to go, Soph. I'll see you soon."

"Okay, but I want you to reserve a night for me next week. I miss you."

"I will," he promised, then he gave her a quick peck on the cheek. "See you soon."

He could feel her eyes on him as he walked out the door and reminded himself that this was not an affair. So why did he feel the slightest bit of regret that he would never go public with their relationship?

Eleven

As good as this thing with her and Ethan turned out to be, Lizzy couldn't help wondering how long it would take the element of newness to wear off. When the sneaking around would become more annoying than exciting.

As it turned out, not long. Barely three weeks.

"Let me take you out to dinner," Ethan said to her that third week when they met at her place on Friday after work. "Anywhere you want to go."

She wanted to. Since that was what normal couples did on a Friday night. They saw films or shows, dined in restaurants. Alone or with friends. She wanted them to have a normal relationship. But the fact was, they didn't. And they never would. He was always dropping hints, reminding her that this was just sex. Just for fun.

"I like staying in," she told him, but it was a lie. She felt just as bored and confined as he did.

"We can go somewhere quiet and out of the way," he said.

Unfortunately there was no place they could go where he wouldn't be recognized. "I want to, but I can't."

He let it drop and they ordered in, like they usually did. The next morning he left for the U.S. to attend a college friend's birthday party.

She'd missed him terribly and could hardly wait to see him when he returned. His flight arrived too late Tuesday night to come see her, so she sat at work all day Wednesday on pins and needles, edgy with anticipation. Thankfully the queen was too excited with her own news to notice. Her physician had been by yesterday and she was already dilated to two centimeters.

"He said it could still be a few weeks," she told Lizzy. "And the cramps I've been feeling are probably Braxton Hicks, but it seems so real all of the sudden. So close."

They sat together in her suite, going through piles and piles of baby clothes, burp cloths and blankets. Sorting and folding them neatly in preparation for the big day.

When the queen's phone rang, Lizzy got up from the sofa to answer it. It was the king. But he didn't want to speak to his wife. He wanted Lizzy.

"Please come down to my office," he said, then hung up the phone. She tried not to feel alarm, but something in his voice told her she should be worried.

Even if something was wrong, that didn't mean it had anything to do with her, she assured herself. It could be anything.

But why didn't he have his secretary summon her? Why make the call himself?

Lizzy, stop it! She was probably reading way more into this than was actually there.

"The king needs me in his office," she told the queen.

If she had any idea what this was about, she didn't let on. She didn't look the least bit concerned. She was too busy folding onesies and sorting them by color and size. "All right. Tell him not to keep you too long, though. We have organizing to do."

She left the queen's suite and walked down the hall to the king's private office, a feeling of dread building in her belly.

She greeted his secretary with a cheery smile, one she didn't return. Not that she'd ever been the warm and fuzzy type. But it wasn't a good sign.

"Go on in," she said. "They're waiting for you."

They? There was someone else in there?

The feeling of dread multiplied and she had the sudden urge to turn and run. Her hand trembled as she turned the knob and opened the door. The king sat at his desk, looking stern and regal, and when she stepped inside, she saw the other person the secretary had been referring to and her heart sank so low she could swear she felt it slither down into her pelvis. Sitting across the room, slouched in a chair, his legs crossed, was Ethan. His body language said he was relaxed and without care. Bored even.

What the heck was going on?

When she spoke, she struggled to keep her voice even, in case this was some kind of test. On the off chance it had nothing to do with her and Ethan and their affair. "You wanted to see me, sir?"

"Close the door, Miss Pryce."

She closed it quietly, trying to read the expression on Ethan's face, and it was obvious, the way he looked her directly in the eye, almost apologetically, that they had been discovered. Despite how careful they had been, somehow the king found out.

"I guess I don't have to tell you why I called you here," the king said sternly.

Lizzy shook her head, feeling sick to her stomach. So nauseous in fact that she was afraid she might lose her lunch right there on his office carpet.

"I also don't have to tell you how this looks for the family. The prince marrying a secretary."

"No, Your Highness, I—" Wait a minute, did he say *marrying?* Did Ethan actually tell him they were getting *married?*

She glanced over at Ethan and he was wearing this look, one that said just go along with it.

"I…I'm sorry," she finished.

"Don't apologize," Ethan said sharply. "You didn't do anything wrong."

The king shot Ethan a stern look, then turned his attention to Lizzy. "The prince tells me that he approached you at the gala, and despite your objections continued to pursue you afterward. Is that true?"

She could barely breathe much less form words, so she nodded. She was still stuck on the word *married*. Ethan couldn't have actually told him they were planning to wed.

"And you let it go on," the king asked. "Despite knowing that it is grounds for dismissal?"

She lowered her eyes to her feet and nodded.

"Like I told you, Phillip," Ethan said. "You can't fight true love."

True love? Did he love her?

"Ethan tells me that he proposed and you are to be married next spring."

Just the thought made her woozy. Though she had no choice but to go along with it. "Yes, sir, next spring."

"At which time you will no longer continue your employment with the royal family?"

Wait a minute. Was he saying that he *wasn't* going to fire her on the spot? That until this so-called wedding she could keep her job? A glimmer of hope sparked a dim light at the end of the very long, dark tunnel she'd gotten herself trapped in.

She swallowed hard and shook her head. "No, sir."

"Ethan tells me that after the wedding you plan to work in the resort. Although I have to say that I don't approve of a member of the royal family being employed anywhere."

A member of the royal family.

Now she was sure she really would be sick. It was like her nightmare coming true. She didn't want to be a member of the royal family. She didn't even want to be engaged! And the weirdest part about all of this was the king's attitude. She would have expected him to rant and protest and insist they end their relationship. Instead he was acting almost as though he *approved*.

Ethan rose to his feet, casual as you please, while she was on the verge of a panic attack. He turned to his brother. "So, are you satisfied now?"

The king nodded. "However, I would have appreciated a bit of warning."

"I think I've made it pretty clear that my life is none of your business," Ethan replied haughtily.

Lizzy could see the king stewing behind dark, brooding eyes. "I'll see that an announcement is made."

Ethan shrugged. "Fine."

Wait, what? *Announcement?* Ethan was going to let him announce an engagement that never happened?

"If we're finished here, I'd like a private word with my fiancée."

The king nodded. "And I'll talk to my wife."

"Let's go, sweetheart," Ethan said, but Lizzy felt rooted to the floor.

When she didn't budge, he took her upper arm and led her out of the king's office and into the hall. She opened her mouth to speak and he whispered sharply, "Not a word until we're alone."

He all but dragged her to the opposite end of the

wing where he kept an office. Once they were inside he shut the door and locked it. Then he turned to her and said firmly, "You need to calm down and let me explain."

Only then did she realize that she was breathing so hard she was practically hyperventilating, and she was shaking all over. "What the bloody hell did you do?"

"Saved your job, that's what." He led her to a chair and she collapsed into it, her legs shaky and weak.

"By telling the king that we're *engaged?*"

"He found out about us. I'm not sure how, but he confronted me today."

"So you told him we're *engaged?*"

"I didn't have a choice, Lizzy."

"What about the truth? That was a choice."

"You think so? What sounds better to you, that we're madly in love and planning to get married, or that we're having a brief, torrid affair?"

She bit her lip. He had a point.

"I figured it was your best shot at keeping your job. After all, how would it look if the king fired his future sister-in-law? His brother's mistress, on the other hand, would be expendable. The scandal would cause too much damage to the family's image."

He was right. If he had told the king the truth, she definitely would have been sacked. Here Ethan was doing everything he could to save her job, at the risk of his already rocky relationship with his brother, and she was acting selfish and ungrateful.

"I'm sorry, Ethan. I should be thanking you, not complaining. I was just caught off guard."

He smiled. "It's okay. I know you like to be in control. I'd have given you advance warning, but there was no time."

"So what do we do now?" she asked. "We can't actually get married."

"Of course not." She should have been relieved, so why did she feel a tinge of disappointment instead? "We'll pretend to be engaged for a while, a couple of months, tops, then we'll amicably split. You get to keep your job, and everyone is happy."

It made sense. And if it meant keeping her job, how could she argue? "That might actually work. Unless, after we split, they fire me anyway. Then what?"

"Then you come to work for me at the resort. Either way, I'll see to it that you come out of this gainfully employed. I promise."

He looked so earnest, so apologetic, she couldn't be angry with him. Everything he'd done, all the lies he'd told his brother, had been for her. And besides, she had gotten herself into this mess. He may of pursued her, but she'd had a thousand opportunities to tell him no. And she didn't. She had wanted this as much as he did.

"I guess this means we don't have to sneak around any longer," she said.

"On the contrary. We need to make this as public as possible. We have to convince everyone that we really are engaged."

She couldn't help thinking that this was fun for him. Not that she believed for an instant that he had done this on purpose. She had been both arrogant and foolish to believe that they could keep their relationship a secret.

And maybe, for a short while at least, being engaged to a gazillionaire prince might be a little bit exciting. To be on the inside, instead of the outside looking in. Maybe she should just let herself enjoy it.

"So, what's our next move?" she asked.

He sat on the edge of his desk. "Well, first we have to see about a ring."

"A *ring?*"

He shrugged. "Can't be engaged without a ring."

"You don't mean a real ring."

"I could get one out of a Cracker Jack box."

"A what?"

He chuckled. "Never mind. But yes, it will be a real one."

"Won't that be expensive?"

He gave her this look, like, *Yeah, so?* She had to remind herself that he was loaded. But that didn't mean she expected him to spend a lot of money on her. "I'll give it back. After we call it off."

"You don't have to. Consider it…a parting gift."

"I don't think I would feel comfortable doing that."

"Tell you what. Why don't we worry about that when the time comes, okay?"

She was a planner. She liked to know what would happen when, and how she would handle it. Indecision made her nuts. But this time she was just going to have to play it by ear. She nodded reluctantly and asked, "Anything else?"

"An engagement party."

Oh, God, she hadn't even thought of that. But the family would be expecting it. They would probably insist. The idea of all those rich and famous people gathered together in her honor made her knees knock. How could they lie to all of those people?

"Don't worry." He slid off the desk, propped his hands on the arms of her chair, leaned in and kissed her. Then he looked her in the eye and said, "It'll be okay. It's all for show. Nothing in our relationship will change."

Maybe that was part of the problem. "What if the family is angry with me?"

"They'll get over it."

"And the other staff. They're going to hate me."

"It doesn't matter what they think."

To him maybe, but these were people she had to work with every day. People who could potentially make her life a waking nightmare if they wanted to. She'd seen other employees ostracized for less. And the queen, what was she going to think? Lizzy could hardly stand the idea of disappointing her. And all for a relationship that was pretend.

"I should get back to work. I wonder if the king talked to the queen yet."

"You know, you're going to have to start calling them by name."

"I don't know that I could ever do that." Especially since this whole engagement was a sham.

"When do you want to go ring shopping?" he asked. "How about if I pick you up at your place around seven?"

"Okay."

"And I'll take you out to dinner."

She nodded numbly.

Ethan walked her back to the queen's suite, kissed her—actually kissed her in the hallway where anyone could see—then left. Left her to fend for herself. She stood in the hall for a moment, trying to work up the nerve to open the door. If the queen was angry or upset, she wasn't sure what she would do.

And there wasn't a damned thing she could do about it, so she might as well just get it over with.

She forced herself to open the door and step inside. The queen was standing at the window, looking out over the gardens, her back to Lizzy. Lizzy's hands shook as she shut the door and said, "Ma'am?"

She turned to Lizzy, her face unreadable. "I just had an interesting talk with Phillip. Is it true?"

Lizzy bit her lip and nodded.

The queen walked slowly toward her. "So, the mystery man you've been seeing is Ethan?"

She felt sick to her stomach again. "I'm sorry I didn't tell you. I understand if you're angry, or you want me to transfer to a different position."

She stopped in front of Lizzy. "There won't be any transfer. But you know what this means, don't you?"

She was afraid to ask.

It happened so fast, it made her head spin. But one second the queen was standing in front of her, and the next she had pulled Lizzy into a bone-crushing hug.

"It means we're going to be sisters!"

Twelve

Lizzy didn't think anything could be worse than disappointing the queen, but she was wrong. The queen's excitement, as she gushed on about planning the engagement party and wedding preparations, was more scathing than any angry words she could have spoken. Guilt burned a hole in Lizzy's gut and made her ears ring. Because it was all a big lie.

And it kept getting worse.

"You have to call me Hannah now," the queen said, but Lizzy just couldn't see herself being comfortable doing that. Maybe if they were really going to be in-laws, but they weren't.

"Ma'am," she started, but the queen shushed her.

"I *insist*. You're family now."

"Only socially. Until the wedding," she forced herself to say. "I just wouldn't feel comfortable addressing you by your name in a professional context."

She thought about that for a second, then said, "I guess that would be all right. For now. But after it's official, you aren't ever allowed to call me *ma'am* or *Your Highness* again. Agreed?"

Lizzy nodded. And feeling it would only be fair to make an effort, said, "And you can call me Lizzy. All my friends and family do."

"Okay, Lizzy." She beamed with happiness. "I am so excited for you! I can't wait to start planning everything. We're going to have so much fun!"

Lizzy forced a smile. "But it should wait until after the baby is born. You don't need any extra stress right now. In fact, we should postpone the engagement party until the baby is at least a few months old, so you've had proper time to heal." At which time she and Ethan would have already called it quits, saving them all a lot of unnecessary trouble.

But the queen quashed that idea. "Nonsense. I'll need maybe a week to recover. And you know how much I love planning parties. In fact, I have a book of invitation samples in my bedroom. I'll go get it, and we can decide which ones you like best."

She dashed excitedly off to the bedroom, as fast as her protruding belly would allow, leaving Lizzy standing helplessly by herself. With any luck, the baby would be born a few weeks late, and by then she and Ethan would be over.

This was all happening so fast, her head was spinning. And she had a blazing headache forming in her temples.

Probably the stress of lying to royalty.

To kill time, she sat on the couch and tackled the basket of baby clothes still sitting there, fluffing and folding the tiny outfits and fuzzy blankets. Preparing for the baby's arrival was the only real thing in her life right now. Everything else felt like a fabrication. And lies were work. They seemed to have a way of snowballing out of control. Of course, besides the engagement, everything Ethan told the king had been true. He had approached her at the gala, and he had been the one to pursue her.

That didn't make her feel any less guilty though.

She was beginning to wonder what was taking the queen so long, when she heard her call, "Eliza— I mean, Lizzy, could you come here, please?" There was a frantic note to her voice that filled Lizzy with alarm. Tossing the blanket she'd been folding aside, she jumped up and sprinted to the bedroom. But she wasn't there. "Ma'am?"

"I'm in the bathroom," she called.

Lizzy walked over and peeked inside. The queen stood at the counter, gripping the edge, a pained look on her face. "Are you okay?"

She looked at Lizzy, then nodded toward the floor, and Lizzy realized she was standing in a puddle. "Oh, my gosh. Is that what I think it is?"

"My water broke. And there is no way that the

contraction I just felt is a Braxton Hicks." She looked over at Lizzy and smiled. "I think I'm in labor!"

The king wanted to go directly to the hospital but the queen, *Hannah,* as Lizzy had been forcing herself to call her all afternoon, wanted to spend the long, painful hours ahead at home. The doctor came by to check her, and suggested she keep moving to get the labor progressing more rapidly, so Lizzy, the king and Princess Sophie all took turns walking the grounds with her, and as the sun began to set, and her contractions grew stronger, they moved the party inside and walked up and down the halls of the residence.

Lizzy had taken off her suit jacket hours ago, and with her feet beginning to throb, she kicked her shoes off and paced in her stocking feet. Something she never could have imagined herself doing under *any* circumstances. She even plucked the pins from her hair and let it tumble down loose. And the weirdest thing about it all? It didn't feel uncomfortable or strange.

It was funny how quickly things could change.

She was so busy helping out that until her cell phone rang at seven, she had completely forgotten that she was supposed to meet Ethan to go ring shopping and out to dinner. She stepped into the queen—Hannah's—bedroom to answer it.

"You stood me up," he said, and joked, "You sick of me *already?*"

"I'm sorry. I meant to call. But it's been a little crazy around her. The queen—Hannah, I mean, is in labor."

"Really? Are you at the hospital?"

"Not yet. She wants to stay home as long as possible."

"Is there anything I can do?"

"Not right now. I'll call you and let you know when we go to the hospital."

"So I guess ring shopping will have to wait."

"Why don't you go without me?"

"Isn't this something we should do together? What if I pick out a ring that you hate?"

"I trust you. Besides, I like surprises."

"No, you don't. You like predictability and order."

He was right. It was creepy that he knew her that well. But comforting in a way, because he didn't use it to exploit her. "I'm sure whatever you get will be perfect."

"If that's what you want," he said, and she could swear she detected a note of disappointment in his voice. But it was better this way. Picking out a ring together would feel too…real. She didn't want to get too swept up in this charade and do something dumb, like fall in love with him.

And even if she did, it would never work. They were too different. Besides, he didn't have time for her.

"What size?" he asked.

"Size?"

"Ring. I want it to fit."

"Oh, a five and a half."

"Five and a half it is. Call me later and I'll meet you at the hospital. I'd like to be there when my first nephew is born."

"I will. I promise. Talk to you later." She disconnected, and turned, startled to see Princess Sophie leaning in the doorway.

"Talking to Ethan?" she asked, then added, "Your fiancé?"

Was she angry? According to the queen—Hannah—Sophie was very protective of Ethan.

Lizzy nodded, wringing her hands. This was turning into the most stressful, topsy-turvy day of her entire life.

"My brother told me. Congratulations."

"Thank you."

Sophie's face split into a grin. "Relax. I don't bite."

"Sorry," she said, her cheeks burning with embarrassment. "I wasn't sure how everyone would take the news. When you thought of Ethan getting married, I'm probably not what you imagined."

"Why would you say that?"

"Not only am I an employee, but as far as I know, I don't have a drop of royal blood in me."

She waved away the notion with a flip of her hand. "That's my brother talking. Phillip, I mean. Personally I think it's great. I've never seen Ethan so happy."

Sophie's words surprised her. "Really?"

"When he first came to us, Ethan was…lost, I guess. He didn't have anyone. Lot's of business associates and friends, and lots of women but no one special. It took quite some time to trust that what he had here was real. Phillip hasn't helped, being so overbearing and judgmental. He means well, but he has the unfortunate tendency to alienate anyone who doesn't see things exactly his way. But lately, Ethan seems to have accepted his position in the family, and the responsibilities of that position."

"I noticed that, too," Lizzy said. It had been weeks since Ethan had had anything negative to say about Phillip.

"The real test," Sophie said, "is going to be if *you* can."

"I'm going to try." At least until this charade was over.

Sophie smiled. "All that really matters is that you love each other."

Oh, God. More guilt to add to the heaping, festering pile.

"And by the way, I really like your hair down," Sophie said. "It's very sexy. You should wear it like that all the time."

Maybe she would.

Philip appeared behind them. "The doctor just checked Hannah again. She's dilated to six centimeters. He said if we keep her moving, it might only be a few more hours."

"I'll go next," Lizzy said, because walking the halls, uttering soothing words, kept her from thinking about the mess she was currently in and the idea that she may be falling in love with Ethan.

She just had to keep telling herself that Ethan knew what he was doing, and everything would eventually turn out all right.

Ethan never realized how long it took for a woman to have a baby. He met Lizzy and Sophie in the royal family's private wing of the hospital around ten, and despite that Hannah had gone into labor nearly nine hours earlier, at midnight they were still sitting there waiting.

When he'd first walked in, Lizzy wasn't there, but Sophie grabbed him and hugged him fiercely. She smelled like apples.

"Congratulations, you big jerk." But it was said with affection. "I can't believe you kept it from me."

Ethan smiled and shrugged. "You know me. I like to keep you on your toes. Where is she?"

"In the loo, I think." She leaned close and whispered, "Between us, of all our staff, Elizabeth has always been one of my favorites. You'll never find one more loyal. I know she'll be a fantastic wife."

"Me, too." He only felt a little guilty for lying.

"I did notice, however, that she isn't wearing a ring."

"Funny you should mention that." He pulled the ring box from the pocket of his slacks and opened it. "The engagement happened a bit abruptly, and I only now got around to it."

Sophie took it from him and examined the sparkling diamond. "What you lacked in timing, you certainly made up for in size. How many karats?"

"Six. The setting is platinum, since the only jewelry I ever see her wear is silver."

She snapped it closed and handed it back. "It's lovely."

"You think she'll like it?"

"I think she'll love it."

He hoped so, since he wouldn't be accepting it back when this was over. He wanted to do something nice for her, since he was the one who had set out to seduce her and now had them engaged. His selfishness had almost cost her a career she'd spent almost ten years building. He could easily relate to that feeling of dread. He experienced it after his partner's embezzling, when he saw everything he'd worked so hard for slipping away before his eyes.

Besides, he was in no rush to end this. He was actually looking forward to the truth being out, the opportunity to have a somewhat normal relationship. And that certainly surprised him.

Lizzy had walked into the room after that, and though he wanted to give her the ring right away, he figured it would be best if he waited until they were alone.

At one-fifteen Phillip stepped through the door to the waiting room, beaming with the smile of a proud new father.

"Eight pounds, eleven ounces, and twenty-three inches long," he bragged. "He and Hannah are both doing great."

"Congratulations!" Sophie squealed, giving him a big hug.

Ethan put their differences aside and gave him a firm handshake. "What's the big guy's name?"

"Frederick," Phillip said. "After our father."

Ethan realized it was the first time Phillip had referred to Ethan as a part of their family. And he was surprised to find that he liked it. Maybe this rift between them was beginning to heal.

"That's a good name," he said.

"Can we see him?" Sophie asked excitedly.

"Of course. Hannah is tired, but excited to show him off."

Sophie turned to Ethan and Lizzy. "Are you coming?"

"Why don't you go first, get some time alone," Ethan told her. "We'll wait out here."

"Are you sure?"

Lizzy smiled. "Go ahead."

When they were gone, Ethan told Lizzy, "I hope you don't mind that I spoke for us both."

She smiled. "That's okay. They should have some family time. But really, you should be in there with them."

He shrugged. "They're not going anywhere. Besides, I'd rather be out here with you."

They reclaimed their seats on the sofa and he pulled her close to him. He wrapped his arms around her and she leaned her head back against his shoulder. They were a good fit. It was comfortable.

"That was really amazing," she said. "Being there to help her through her labor. It was a little scary. She was in a lot of pain. But I guess we all have to go through it eventually, and it's better to know what's coming than to be surprised."

He wondered if she meant that she wanted kids. He'd never asked, and she'd never brought it up. "You want them? Kids, I mean."

"Someday."

He couldn't see her face, but her voice sounded a little wistful.

"How about you?" she asked.

"I don't know. I never really thought about it. I can't see that I would ever have time to be a father."

He wondered, if he and Lizzy were to have children, what they would look like. Would they have her fair coloring or his darker features? Would they have her petite stature, or take after his side of the family and be tall? Would they have boys or girls, or a few of each? God, where did those thoughts come from? He didn't want kids. Not with Lizzy or anyone else.

They sat in silence for several minutes, and Lizzy's breathing had become slow and even. She'd looked utterly exhausted when he'd arrived at ten. She had to be beyond tired now. "You still with me?"

"Sort of," she said in a sleepy voice.

"Do you want me to take you home?"

She sighed and curled against him, snuggling herself up to his chest. "Not until I see the baby."

"I have something for you."

She yawned. "Oh, yeah?"

"I went shopping tonight."

That seemed to wake her. She sat up and said, "You did?"

She looked so excited, it made him smile. This might not have been real, but that didn't mean they couldn't enjoy it. "You want to see?"

She nodded eagerly.

He pulled the box from his pocket and handed it to her. But for a second she just held it. "Aren't you going to open it?"

"Before I look, I wanted to thank you again for everything you did today. For saving my job."

"It's okay." It wasn't a hardship. "Open it."

She took a deep breath and flipped the lid open. Her eyes settled on the ring and her breath caught. For what felt like a full minute she just sat there staring at it, not uttering a word.

"Well?" he asked.

"It's amazing," she said, finally peeling her eyes from the stone to look at him. "It's the most beautiful thing I've ever seen."

He grinned. "You don't think it's too small?"

"Small?" she asked incredulously. "What is this, fifteen karats?"

"Only six."

"Only six. The ring that Roger got me had a stone so tiny it couldn't even be measured in karats. It was a fleck of dust compared to this."

"Let's see if it fits." He took the box from her and

lifted the ring from its velvet bed. She held out her hand and he slipped it on. Perfect.

She shifted her hand in the light, making the stone shimmer. "It's so beautiful. But it's too much, Ethan."

"Lizzy, I can afford it. And I'm probably going to be spending a fair amount of money on you in the next few weeks, so you'd better get used to it."

She opened her mouth to object—at least he assumed it was going to be an objection—but the door opened and Sophie poked her head out.

"She's asking for you."

Thirteen

Lizzy thought that Hannah looked like an angel, sitting up in bed, the baby swaddled in blue and cradled in her arms. She had never seen her look more beautiful or content. Or happy.

She smiled brightly when Lizzy and Ethan walked in the room. "Come see him."

Lizzy walked to her bedside, Ethan behind her, and Hannah held him out so they could see. He was round and pink with a shock of jet-black hair. His eyes were open and alert, and a deep, clear blue. He looked just like his daddy.

"He's beautiful," Lizzy said.

"Do you want to hold him?"

She nodded eagerly, and Hannah set him in her

arms. He smelled of baby powder and soap. She touched his tiny fingers and they curled around hers.

She had this sudden sensation, this intense feeling of longing deep down inside her.

She wanted this. She wanted what Hannah had. Marriage to a man who adored her. A family. She wanted it so much she ached. She wanted this with Ethan.

You're just caught up in the moment, she told herself. And loopy from lack of sleep. What she wasn't thinking about was the midnight feedings and sleepless nights. The spitting up and dirty diapers. The *responsibility.* She liked her freedom and she wasn't ready to give that up. Not for anyone. "He's perfect," she said.

"And already stubborn," Hannah joked. "I had to push for almost two hours."

"I think he gets that from you," Phillip teased.

The king was so quiet and serious all of the time. It was strange to see him so relaxed and personable. But Lizzy liked it. Even though at some point she would go back to being just another employee, and he would go back to being her employer and any friendliness between them would cease.

She turned to Ethan. "You want to hold him?"

He put out his arms and she set the baby in them. He looked a little awkward, like someone who wasn't accustomed to holding a baby.

"He's so tiny," Ethan said.

"He didn't feel tiny on the way out," Hannah said.

"I can't imagine how much bigger he would have been if I'd carried him to term."

Ethan touched his little fingers and his lips and his button nose, and something in Lizzy's heart shifted almost imperceptibly. If they had a baby, that would be the way Ethan looked at it and held it.

Stop it, Lizzy!

What the heck was wrong with her? It was one thing to get sentimental, but this was over the top.

Hannah yawned deeply and Phillip said, "We should let you get some sleep."

"You both must be exhausted." Ethan handed the baby to him, and it was the closest Lizzy had ever seen them. They looked so similar it gave her chills. And she hoped after this they might start acting like real brothers.

Phillip handed the baby back to Hannah and said, "I'll walk you out."

He walked with them to the waiting room and stood with Lizzy while Ethan stopped in the restroom.

"Long day," he said, and she nodded. "I expect you to take tomorrow off." He looked at his watch. "Or should I say today."

"I will." For once she didn't mind the idea of missing work. News would get around of their engagement, and God only knows how the other palace employees were going to take it.

He touched her arm, and she was so surprised, she almost flinched. "I wanted to thank you for all your help today."

"Of course, sir."

"It meant a lot to my wife," he said, then added, "And to me."

"It was a pleasure."

"And I'm sorry if I was harsh yesterday afternoon. I'm sure Ethan has told you that we don't see eye to eye on everything."

That was an understatement. "He may have mentioned that."

"I'm hardheaded, I'll admit it, but I try to be fair."

"I know, sir."

"Ethan is different since he met you."

Was he? "Different how?"

"He's less belligerent. He seems…settled. He's ready for this."

Was he trying to convince himself, or her? If she didn't know any better, she might suspect that Phillip knew the truth about this so-called engagement. But how could he?

He gave her arm a squeeze, then let go. "I should get back. If I don't kick Sophie out she'll stay all night. Get some sleep."

"You, too, sir."

He started to walk away, then turned back. "When we're not at work, you can call me Phillip."

"Okay," she said, and forced herself to say, "Phillip."

It was very…odd.

He smiled. "Good night, Lizzy."

He disappeared through the door, and she realized

she was smiling, too. This had been a really good day. A weird, confusing day. But a good one.

"What was that about?" Ethan asked from behind her.

She turned to him, half-tempted to tell him what Phillip said, but decided against it. "Nothing. We were just talking."

"Ready to go?"

"Am I ever. I'm exhausted."

"Am I just dropping you off, or would you like company?"

Considering her state of mind, it would be much better if she went to bed alone, but she didn't want to be alone. Knowing she was asking for trouble, she smiled and said, "I would love some company."

Ethan spent the night, and they slept in late, then they showered and he took her out to lunch. Out of her apartment, in a real restaurant, where there were other people. And it was so nice not having to worry about being seen. Due to the headlines in the local morning papers—the birth of the king's first son and the prince's engagement—everyone seemed to notice them. They must have heard a dozen congratulations and well wishes.

She wasn't used to being the center of attention. To being noticed at all. And it wasn't as bad as she anticipated. A little strange, but she had the feeling her entire life would be strange for quite some time.

When they pulled onto her street later, it was clear just how strange.

Outside her building was a crowd of reporters and news vans so vast the entire street was blocked and the police had been called to direct traffic.

"Oh, my God." She stared with her mouth hanging open.

"I thought this might happen," Ethan said.

"How did they even know where I live?"

"They're the press." As though that were reason enough. And he was probably right. The press in Morgan Isle was only slightly less aggressive and vicious than in England.

"I can't believe this."

"Does your building have a back entrance?"

She shook her head. The only way in was through them.

When he got to the intersection just before her building he swung a sharp left and zipped down the road in the opposite direction.

"Where are we going?"

"My place. You can stay there until this dies down."

"How long?"

"Just a day or two."

"I don't have any clothes with me. And what about work?"

"Do you really feel like dealing with that mob?"

She sighed. "No, not really."

"I can send one of my people over to get some clothes for you."

That would be too weird. Some stranger rooting around in her things. "I can have my friend Maddie do it. She has a key."

She pulled out her cell phone and tried calling Maddie but she didn't answer. She was sure she had probably already heard the news. And knowing Maddie's opinion of the royal family, she might be upset with Lizzy. She left her a message asking her to call as soon as she got in, then used her cell phone to call her voice mail. There were a couple dozen messages. From reporters mostly. Everyone wanted an exclusive on her rags-to-riches story. She deleted them all. There was also a message from her mother, and one from each of her sisters. She saved those to listen to them later. The only time they ever called was when they wanted or needed something. And when they got what they wanted, they would cut all ties again.

No doubt they were seeing this as their ticket out of the public housing project.

It took the entire fifteen-minute drive across town to Ethan's building on the coast to wade through all the messages, and she had half a mind to call the phone company and have her number changed.

Ethan pulled up to the underground garage, punched in a code, and the door raised. The spots were filled with sports cars and other expensive luxury imports. He parked in a spot right by the elevator and they climbed out. Inside the elevator he pressed the button for the top floor. It rose without stopping and opened into a hallway outside a set of double doors.

He opened the door, stepping aside so she could enter. Her first impression was the sheer size of the apartment, and the fact that it was painfully modern. The kitchen, dining area and living room were one large open space with a cathedral ceiling and it was all decorated in a pallet of black, white, chrome, glass and stainless steel. It desperately needed a woman's touch.

"This is it," he said. "Home sweet home."

"It's…nice."

He shut the door behind them. "It's cold and impersonal, but I'm only leasing until I find something more permanent."

She set her purse down on the glass entry table next to the door. "It's very clean."

"I'm not here much. And I have a housekeeper who comes in Monday, Wednesday and Friday. You want a tour?"

"There's more?"

He grinned. "Four bedrooms, my office and four baths."

"Well, let's see it then."

The rest of the rooms were decorated very much the same way. And his bedroom alone was larger than her entire apartment. What could one person need with all of this space? Of course, if she had money to burn, and could hire a housekeeper to keep it up, who's to say she wouldn't live somewhere like this.

They had just finished the tour and were still

standing in his bedroom when her cell phone rang. It was Maddie.

"I have to take this," she said.

"You want some privacy?"

"Is that all right?"

"Of course. Make yourself at home. I'll go open us a couple of beers."

"Sounds good."

He left, shutting the bedroom door behind him, and she answered her phone. "Hey, Maddie. I'll bet you're wondering what's going on."

"How could you, Lizzy? How could you go sneaking around behind everyone's backs. And with a man like that? Don't you have any pride?"

She could hear by her voice that she was just as hurt as she was angry. "It's not what you think. And besides, I wanted to tell you, but I couldn't."

"Are you pregnant?"

"No, of course not!"

"Then why would you marry someone like him? You know that he's using you."

"It's not like that."

"You think he actually loves you? Well, he doesn't."

Maddie was right about that. And it pained Lizzy to know that. Lizzy owed her the truth. She trusted her not to tell anyone. "It's not about love. And we're not really getting married."

"What do you mean? It's all over the papers."

Starting from the night of the gala, all the way to yesterday afternoon, Lizzy told her the entire story.

"So he did it to save your job?" Maddie asked incredulously, as though she couldn't believe someone like Ethan could have a decent bone in his body.

"And he's letting me stay at his place until the media swamping my apartment goes away. Unfortunately, I don't have any clothes with me."

"Just tell me what you need. I'll bring it to you."

She gave her a list of clothes and toiletries she would need. "Thank you so much, Maddie. And I'm sorry I didn't tell you the truth. The whole thing just sort of snowballed out of control."

"I shouldn't have been so harsh."

"It's okay."

"No, it isn't. I guess you could say my opinion of the royal family is somewhat jaded."

"Why, Maddie? What has anyone ever done to you?" The instant the words were out of her mouth, she knew. Before Maddie even said a word.

"You know how the former king used to be with new female employees," Maddie said.

"Oh, Maddie."

"Everyone warned me about him. But I thought I was different. I though I meant something to him. But he used me. I never told anyone what happened. I was too ashamed."

"Maddie, I'm so sorry."

"It was my own fault, Lizzy. And I didn't want to see you make the same mistake."

"Phillip and Ethan are nothing like their father. They're good people."

"It was a long time ago, and I should let it go. I'm going to try."

That was all Lizzy could ask. And maybe finally talking about it would help her move on.

"Just do me a favor," Maddie said.

"What? Anything."

"Whatever you do, don't fall in love with him."

"I won't," she promised, but she couldn't deny it even if she tried. She had fallen in love with Ethan. Now she had to figure out a way to fall back out again.

Fourteen

Work Monday morning was a strange experience for Lizzy. Reactions from the other employees were varied. Some of the older, more experienced people gave her scathing looks or the cold shoulder, while some of the younger office girls regarded her with envy. But she was so busy in the following weeks, she really didn't have time to concern herself with it.

A week after the announcement, the mob outside her building still hadn't cleared, then one of her neighbors came in late one night and caught a stranger hanging around Lizzy's apartment door. He was scared off, but when the police arrived, they found that the lock had been tampered with. Because her building had no security, Phillip and Hannah insisted she find a safer place to live. Unfortunately that sort of place wasn't exactly in her budget. They offered her a room at the palace, but Ethan surprised her by saying that she would be staying with him.

"Are you sure?" she asked him when they were alone.

"It's fine," Ethan assured her, and surprisingly, he seemed to mean it. Even weirder, she *liked* living with him and they slipped easily into a routine. She didn't even mind having someone else doing her laundry or cleaning up after her, and Ethan's house-keeper was a fantastic cook. Even the attention from the public was getting easier, though she didn't think she would ever get completely used to it. Not that she would have to. She knew Ethan wasn't in love with her and this wasn't going to last. But she could enjoy her new life.

As the days turned to weeks, and the weeks into almost two months, Ethan made no mention of when this fake engagement would come to an end. Just yesterday he informed her that he'd purchased tickets for the opera in late September, almost two months away, and he brought up the idea of them taking a trip to the States together for the holidays.

"I don't know what I'll do when you leave," Hannah had begun telling her. "My life will fall apart."

And for the first time she began to wonder if may-be her days as a palace employee were numbered. Maybe she would be taking that job in the resort

Ethan had mentioned. Since she couldn't imagine ever not working.

"I can train a replacement."

"I'm just being selfish," Hannah said. "I think it's wonderful about you and Ethan. I've never seen him so content. And you're positively glowing."

Lizzy's heart flipped over in her chest. "Glowing?"

Hannah nodded. "You look radiant. And that's a definite sign of a woman in love."

According to Lizzy's mom, it was the sign of something else, too. Hadn't her mom told her the story a million times of how, when she was pregnant with Lizzy, everyone used to comment on how her skin glowed. She said it was the best she'd ever looked in her life.

But that was ridiculous. Her period was a few days late, but that wasn't unusual for her, and she was sure they used protection every time. Didn't they? Of course they did. Although she had been feeling especially tired the last few days…

No, it wasn't possible. It couldn't be.

"Lizzy, are you okay?" Hannah asked, concern in her eyes. "All the color just drained from your face."

Lizzy forced a smile. "I'm fine. Just feeling a little woozy all of a sudden."

"Sit down."

Her legs were feeling a little shaky, so she sank down onto the sofa. She was being silly. There was no way she was pregnant. It was impossible.

"Can I get you anything?" Hannah asked.

She shook her head. The wooziness was subsiding, but there was a feeling of dread building inside her. She knew she wouldn't be able to relax until she knew for sure. "I'm feeling better."

"Even so, maybe you should take the rest of the day off."

In the nine years she had worked in the palace she had never left early for any reason. Not even when she was going through her divorce and it felt as though her entire world was crashing down around her.

Not until today.

"You know, I think I will."

Though she knew it was a waste of money, Lizzy stopped at the pharmacy on the way home from work. She wasn't pregnant. She *knew* she wasn't.

When she got to Ethan's, she set her purchase on the table. Thankfully he wouldn't be home for several hours, and it was the housekeeper's day off. Deliberately taking her time, she put water on for tea and checked her voice mail for messages. She wasn't in a rush, because the test was really only a formality.

She waited for the water to boil and fixed her tea just the way she liked it, with plenty of cream and sugar, and took a few sips.

No rush. Just taking her time.

Using the master bath, she took the test, following the directions to the letter, then sat the convenient little wand on the counter facedown and waited for the results. The directions said two minutes, but she waited four just to be sure. She turned it over, assuring herself it was going to be negative, and looked at the convenient little indicator window where it would say *Pregnant* or *Not Pregnant.* For several long seconds she stared at it, to be sure it wasn't a trick of the light.

She was pregnant with Ethan's baby.

For a moment she was too stunned to think straight, to even breathe. Then she started to get this feeling. It began as a tingle in her belly, then it slowly worked it's way outward. To her arms and legs, then her fingers and toes, and though it took a moment to register, she realized finally that what she was feeling was excitement.

She was pregnant, and she was…happy. But how would Ethan feel?

Surprised at first, she was sure, but considering how close they had become, and how well they got along, he couldn't possibly see this as anything but a blessing. Could he? He'd been talking less and less about the temporary nature of their relationship. Not that he'd come right out and said he wanted a commitment, or that he loved her, but all the signs were there. Weren't they?

She would just have to figure out a way to break it to him gently.

It shouldn't take more than a day. Two tops. Then she would definitely tell him. And when she did, she knew that everything would be okay.

* * *

Something was up with Lizzy.

The past couple of weeks she had been acting… different. Ethan couldn't quite put his finger on the change, and when he'd asked if something was wrong, she swore that everything was fine. But he wasn't buying it.

He was beginning to suspect that this relationship had become more than just sex—for both of them. Which meant things would start to get complicated, to interfere with his work—hell, they already were— and that was a luxury he could not afford. He had just got his professional life back on track.

Which had him thinking that maybe it was time to end this charade and go their separate ways. But it never seemed like the right time, and every time he tried, something stopped him. He just didn't feel ready to let her go. And the longer he waited, the harder it would be. Every day he thought, tomorrow, then tomorrow would come, and she would do or say something to endear her to him even more, and he would completely lose his nerve.

His biggest mistake had been letting her stay at his flat. He should have encouraged her to accept Phillip and Hannah's offer to stay at the palace. It had been a knee-jerk decision. One that he was sure would come back to bite him in the behind. And the following morning, the depth of that wound became all too clear.

Lizzy had already left for work. Ethan was on his way out the door when he heard her cell phone ring, and realized she'd left it on the table by the door. When he checked the display, it was a palace number.

"You forgot your phone," he said, in lieu of a hello, and heard her groan.

"Bugger. I'd forget my head if it wasn't attached. I don't suppose you'll be at the palace today."

He hadn't planned on it, but he could make the time. Since it was very likely that their time was limited. "I might be able to drop it off later this afternoon."

He could feel her smile through the phone line. "If you do, it just might earn you something extra special tonight."

Which meant he was definitely in for a treat. Meaning that talk they were going to have to have would be postponed at least another day. "I have a meeting at eleven. How about one-thirty?"

"Perfect. We could have lunch together."

"Sure," he said, before he could think better of it. The more time they spent together, the harder it was going to be to let go. But what harm could one lunch do? "I'll see you then."

"See you then," she said, then disconnected.

He slipped her phone into his jacket pocket and let himself out of the flat. He punched the button for the elevator, and while he waited, Lizzy's phone rang a second time. The number on the display was unfamiliar, but in case it was something important, he answered.

"I'm calling from Pearson's pharmacy to let Ms.

Pryce know that her physician's office phoned in her prescription."

Prescription? Was Lizzy sick? The swift feeling of alarm caught him by surprise. If there was something wrong, she would have told him, wouldn't she?

He knew it was none of his business, but he asked anyway. "Which prescription is that?"

"Her prenatal vitamins."

It took a moment for her words to register, and when they did, their meaning hit him like a sucker punch. Then he realized it had to be a mistake. A mix-up at the pharmacy. "Are you sure?"

"Quite sure, sir. They're ready to be picked up."

"I…I'll tell her, thank you." He disconnected, too stunned to think straight, to process the information. There was only one reason he knew of that a woman would take prenatal vitamins.

Lizzy was pregnant.

It was barely nine-thirty when Lizzy's office door opened and Ethan stepped inside. She greeted him with a smile and said, "You're early." And when he didn't return the smile, her heart dropped. "What's wrong?"

He closed the door and turned to her. "You don't know?"

Oh, my gosh, had someone died? Was something wrong with Frederick? A million possibilities raced through her mind in the instant it took her to rise from her chair. "Tell me."

"The pharmacy called this morning," he said. "Your prescription is ready."

Uh-oh.

Her heart sank even deeper in her chest. *Don't panic just yet,* she told herself. It was entirely possible that he didn't know what the prescription was for. *Maybe he's just worried that you might be sick.*

Then he tossed a small white bag onto her desk. "I took the liberty of picking it up for you."

Oh, God.

"Is there something you neglected to tell me?" he asked.

Once again, she'd waited so long to tell him the truth that he'd found out for himself. And she had to try to explain why she had essentially lied to him. Her mouth was suddenly so dry she could barely peel her tongue from the roof of her mouth to speak. And when she did, her voice came out as a croak. "I was going to tell you."

"So it's true," he said, and it was clear that he was upset with her. Not that she blamed him. She only hoped that he was upset that she'd lied, not that she was pregnant. She wanted him to be happy about becoming a father.

She nodded and said, "I'm pregnant."

"How long have you known?"

"Just a couple of weeks." But it might as well have been a lifetime. She should have told him right away. The day she took the test. "I should have told you. I'm sorry. I did try. I just…" She shrugged. "I just didn't know what to say."

"How did this happen?" he asked. His voice was calm and even. *Too* patient.

"I don't know. We've always been careful."

Ethan cursed under his breath, a really bad sign.

"I know that neither of us was expecting this, and at first I was pretty freaked out, too. I love my career, and my freedom, but the more time I've had to think about it, the more I see it as a blessing."

Something in Ethan's face said he didn't see it as a blessing.

He just needed time, she told herself. A day or two to let it sink in, then everything would be fine. Then he would be just as happy as she was.

"I need to ask you something, and I want the truth," he said.

"Okay."

He looked her directly in the eye and asked, "Did you do this on purpose?"

She was so stunned by his words, she couldn't speak. That he would even suggest such a thing was so far out of her realm of comprehension, she could only stare at him with her mouth hanging open.

"The truth, Lizzy."

She'd never seen his eyes so cold, or heard his voice so devoid of emotion. And when she finally found her own voice, it came out unusually high-pitched. "Are you serious?"

"Just tell me. Yes or no."

Only then did everything become crystal clear. He didn't want the baby. And even worse, he didn't want her. It was all a charade to him. Their engagement. All the time they had been spending together. He was only playing a role.

She had never felt so cheap, so *used* in her entire life. Maddie had been right. Despite his claims to be different, Ethan was a royal through and through. And no different than his father.

"What did you expect?" he asked. "Did you really think I would be happy about this?"

Foolishly, she had. "Get out."

He just stared at her.

"I mean it, Ethan." Her voice rose in pitch. She didn't even care that anyone in the main office might hear. She just needed to be alone to think. "Leave, right now."

And he did, without saying another word. She even managed to wait until the door closed behind him before she completely fell apart.

Fifteen

Ethan got in his car and drove. For hours, going nowhere in particular. And the longer he drove, the more painfully aware he became of the fact that he was a jerk.

He had dragged Lizzy into this relationship, wheedled his way into her life, then had the gall to be mad at her for wanting to protect her feelings.

What the hell was wrong with him?

That was easy. The intensity and depth of his feelings for Lizzy scared the hell out of him. When they were keeping things casual, when he knew she wasn't interested in a commitment, he'd had no trouble. Even the ribbing he'd been getting from

Charles about the engagement hadn't bothered him. Because in his mind, it still wasn't real.

The look on Lizzy's face when he'd asked her if she'd done it on purpose. He'd never seen her look like that. So devastated and hurt. And disappointed. But how was he supposed to act? She'd been keeping this child from him. Even after he'd moved her into his penthouse, into his *life*.

So she wasn't perfect. Well, neither was he. And like it or not, they were going to have to work this out.

Instead of driving home, where he would have to face Lizzy, he found himself back at the palace. It was late, the palace dark and quiet. He roamed the halls for a while, studying the portraits of his ancestors. His family. Though he always saw a resemblance in looks, he never really felt as though he belonged. Maybe he felt as though, if he accepted his role in the family, his *proper* place, the person he had been—his mother's son—would cease to exist.

But lately, since he'd met Lizzy, he'd let his guard down. He had started to feel more accepted. He'd let it happen. And the truth was, he liked himself now more than he ever had before.

As Ethan walked back down the stairs, he noticed a light on in the study. Curious, he walked over to the door and looked in, surprised to find Phillip there, reading a book, his son asleep on his shoulder.

He knocked lightly on the door and Phillip looked up, surprised to see him, too. "Ethan. Is something wrong?"

"Am I disturbing you?"

"No. I'm trying to let Hannah get some sleep." He set his book down. "Frederick has been fussy the last few nights. He prefers to be held."

"Don't you have a nanny for this sort of thing?"

A nerve in his jaw ticked. "I was raised by a nanny. My children will know their father loves them."

His honesty threw Ethan for a second. "Are you saying our father didn't love you?"

"If he did, he never showed it." Phillip gestured to the sofa and Ethan sat down. "I assume there's a reason you're here and not with Lizzy?"

He almost told Phillip to mind his own business. A knee-jerk reaction. Then it registered that Phillip was asking not to control or manipulate him, but because he cared. "We had a fight," he admitted.

"Your first?"

"Actually, yeah." Up until tonight, they'd barely had so much as a difference of opinion. That had to say something, didn't it?

"She's pregnant?" Phillip asked, surprising Ethan once again.

For an instant he wondered if Phillip had planted listening devices in his apartment, but that would be over the top even for him. This wasn't a covert operation. This was just family. Ethan's family. "How did you know?"

"Hannah guessed. She mentioned something about Lizzy glowing, and Lizzy went white as a sheet."

"Glowing?"

Phillip shrugged. "Don't ask me. But apparently Lizzy knew what she meant."

"It must be one of those female things us guys aren't meant to understand."

"One of many." The baby shifted and made a soft noise of protest, so Phillip shifted him to the opposite shoulder and patted his back gently.

In seven months or so, Ethan would be doing the same thing. And at the moment instead of freaking him out, the idea of being a father felt settling somehow.

"So," Phillip asked, "are you going to ask her to marry you?"

He opened his mouth to answer him, then the meaning of his words sunk in. As far as Phillip knew, he had already asked. At least, that's what Ethan thought. Apparently he'd been wrong about that, too. "You knew that the engagement was a sham?"

Phillip nodded, and though he could have been smug about it, he wasn't.

"How long did you know? About me and Lizzy, I mean."

"I recognized her that night at the gala."

So he knew the entire time? And never said a word? Ethan shook his head in disbelief. And all the while Ethan had strut around, foolishly believing that he had gotten the best of his brother. How could he have been so blindly arrogant? So childish?

He chose Lizzy, at least in part, because he believed Phillip would disapprove. But the joke was on Ethan. Not only did Phillip approve, but somewhere along the way Ethan had gone and fallen in love.

Yes, he realized, he loved her.

"Did you really think I wouldn't be keeping close tabs on my investment?" Phillip asked.

Ethan wanted to be offended, but in all honesty, put in his brother's position, he probably would have done the same thing. "I figured you would disapprove."

"Call me sentimental, but I thought she might be good for you."

"So why confront me?"

"It was beginning to look as though things were getting serious. I was going to tell you that you either needed to end the affair or make a commitment. But then you claimed to be engaged, and I thought it might be fun to let you hang yourself with your own rope. It was a noble act, though. Sacrificing yourself to save her job. I gained a great amount of respect for you that day."

Ethan felt like an idiot. "I'm sorry, Phillip, for the way I've acted. I haven't shown you the respect you deserve."

"No, you haven't, but I haven't exactly made your life easy, either. I had to know that I could trust you. And I supposed I unfairly blamed your mother for our father's infidelity. But it's not as if she was the first. Or the last. Just convenient, I suppose."

"Can we call a truce?"

"I think that would be good idea."

It was more of a relief than Ethan could have imagined. And if not for Lizzy, he might still be the same pigheaded man who seemed to think the world owed him. Maybe it was just that he'd been jealous of Phillip for having a father. Something Ethan had always wanted. He had hated and resented the queen for taking that from him, and transferred that hate to her son. But now it seemed as though Ethan may have been better off never knowing him.

"Do you think there could be others?" Ethan asked.

"Others?"

"Illegitimate heirs."

Phillip shrugged. "It's possible, I suppose. But unless they come forward, we may never know."

"I'd like to look."

"Why?"

Ethan shrugged. He didn't know why it was suddenly important to him to know. It just was. "I guess, lately, the idea of family has taken on new meaning."

"It could mean more scandal for the family. More bad press."

"It could also mean getting to know a brother or sister we didn't know we had. But I won't do it without your blessing."

Phillip considered that for a moment, then said, "Do it."

"You're sure?"

He nodded. "You have my blessing. Just keep me apprised of what you find before you make any contacts."

"I will."

"You know, Ethan, I learned the hard way that when you find something good, you hang on to it."

"You mean Lizzy?"

Phillip nodded. "Do you love her?"

He did. He knew it all along, he just wouldn't let himself see it. "Yes, I do."

"And she loves you?"

"Yeah, she does. At least I think she does."

"Then you should probably try groveling. It worked for me."

The idea of Phillip groveling to win Hannah was a humbling thought, and it made Ethan feel at least a little less inept. And if groveling was what it was going to take, that was what he would do.

Ethan half expected Lizzy to be gone when he pulled into the garage, but her car was there. At least she hadn't bailed on him. Not that he would have blamed her if she had.

But as he stepped inside the flat, he almost tripped over the bags piled there. It looked as though she was completely packed. He should have expected as much, but for some reason the reality of it still stung. Because he honestly didn't want her to go. He could scarcely imagine his life without her in it.

He shut the door quietly behind him and went looking for her.

He found her in the master bath, her makeup and

toiletries in a pile on the vanity. Her eyes looked red, as though she had been crying, but her face was somber. Determined even.

She must have heard him come in, because the sound of his voice when he spoke didn't startle her. "You're leaving?"

She didn't look at him. She just piled everything into a small case and zipped it shut. "That shouldn't surprise you."

"What if I said that I don't want you to go?"

She stared at her hands, which he noticed were trembling. "I'd tell you that it's too late."

She didn't mean that, even though she wanted him to think she did. Apparently this was the part where he did the groveling.

He took a step closer. "Suppose I told you that I love you."

He waited for a reply, instead she grabbed her case and brushed past him. She wasn't going to cut him any slack.

He followed her into the living room. "You can't tell me you don't love me."

"What difference does it make?" She tucked the makeup bag into the front pocket of one of the suitcases. "Nothing about this relationship makes sense."

"When do relationships ever make sense?"

She turned to him, her eyes full of confusion. "I keep thinking about this thing we have. Going over and over it in my head. Trying to figure out how we got here. To this place."

"What place?"

"*Together.* We may have both gone into this not wanting a commitment, but somewhere along the way, it just happened."

"I guess we just never talked about it."

"Not talking about the future doesn't stop it from coming."

She was right. Their future had happened. And it had been such a gradual, smooth transition, he had never noticed.

"You know, I used to think you were the perfect woman for me. Beautiful, funny, fantastic in bed. And as relationship-phobic as I am."

She frowned. "And now you think I'm not the perfect woman for you?"

"Now I *know* you are. It's just that my reasons for thinking so were off. At least, one of them was." He took a step toward her, then another, and when he touched her, she didn't try to stop him. Then he pulled her to him and she practically melted in his arms, then he knew, the bravado was just for show. "I love you, Lizzy, and I want to make this work."

She clung to him, burying her face against his shirt, so that her voice came out muffled when she said, "I do, too."

"Which part?"

She looked up at him and smiled. "Both. I love you Ethan. I didn't mean for it to happen, but it did anyway."

"But there is one problem," he said.

A crease formed in her brow. "What problem?"

"I won't let my son or daughter grow up feeling like I did."

"Like what?"

"Illegitimate. Incomplete. Which means I'm going to have to figure out a way to get you to marry me. For real this time."

The hint of a smile curled the corners of her mouth. "You could ask. I mean, how hard could it be?" She held up her hand. "I've already got the ring."

"You must be forgetting, you told me you would never marry a royal. Too suffocating and claustrophobic, I believe were your exact words. And I'm a royal. Even if I only just realized it."

She took a deep breath and blew it out, as though giving the matter intense consideration, but there was a smile in her eyes. "Well, I suppose, since you're technically only *half*-royal, just this one time I could make an exception."

"You *suppose?*"

She grinned. "Why don't you just ask already and find out?"

He knelt down in front of her. Properly, on one knee. May as well give her the full treatment. She'd more than earned it.

He reached for her, and when she slipped her hand in his he realized she was trembling. He wasn't sure if she was scared, or excited or maybe a bit of both. The only thing he did know for sure was that this was right.

"This is good," he said, and she smiled down at him. "This is really good."

"Yes, it is."

"Lizzy, will you marry me?"

She let loose everything she'd been holding back, threw her arms around his neck and hugged him. "Of course I will!"

He scooped her up and kissed her, never so sure of anything in his life, and amazed that since the day he'd met her, his life hadn't been the same.

"I have an idea," she said, nibbling his lower lip and threading her fingers through his hair. "Since we're getting married eventually anyway, why don't we start the honeymoon right now?"

He laughed and carried her in the direction of the bedroom, because honestly, he was thinking the same thing. "The sooner the better."

* * * * *

Don't miss SOPHIE'S STORY
Book 3 in Michelle Celmer's
ROYAL SEDUCTIONS *series,*
available October 2008
from Silhouette Desire

BRIANNA stretched out beside Ewan, languid as a cat, and promptly fell asleep. Midday sunshine streamed into the chamber, bathing her lovely, long-limbed body in golden light, the sea-scented breeze wafting inside to dry the damp red-gold tendrils curling about her flushed face. Propping himself up on one elbow, Ewan slid his gaze over her. She looked beautiful and whole, satisfied and sated, and altogether happier than he had so far seen her. A slight smile curved her beautiful lips as though she must be in the midst of a lovely dream. She'd molded her lush, lovely body to his and laid her head in the curve of his shoulder and settled in to sleep beside him. For the longest while he lay there turned toward her, content to watch her sleep, at near perfect peace.

Not wholly perfect, for she had yet to answer his marriage proposal. Still, she wanted to make a baby with him, and Ewan no longer viewed her plan as the travesty he once had. He wanted children—sons to carry on after him, though a bonny little daughter with flame-colored hair would be nice, too. But he also wanted more than to simply plant his seed and be on his way. He wanted to lie beside Brianna night upon night as she increased, rub soothing unguents into the swell of her belly, knead the ache from her back and make slow, gentle love to her. He wanted to hold his newly born child in his arms and look down into Brianna's tired but radiant face and blot the perspiration from her brow and be a husband to her in every way.

He gave her a gentle nudge. "Brie?"

"Hmmm?"

She rolled onto her side and he captured her against his chest. One arm wrapped about her waist, he bent to her ear and asked, "Do you think we might have just made a baby?"

Her eyes remained closed, but he felt her tense against him. "I don't know. We'll have to wait and see."

He stroked his hand over the flat plane of her belly. "You're so small and tight it's hard to imagine you increasing."

"All women increase no matter how large or small they start out. I may not grow big as a croft, but I'll be big enough, though I have hopes I may not waddle like a duck, at least not too badly."

The reference to his fair-day teasing was not lost on him. He grinned. "Brianna MacLeod grown so large she must sit still for once in her life. I'll need the proof of my own eyes to believe it."

Despite their banter, he felt his spirits dip. Assuming they were so blessed, he wouldn't have the chance to see her thus. By then he would be long gone, restored to his clan according to the sad bargain they'd struck. He opened his mouth to ask her to marry him again and then clamped it closed, not wanting to spoil the moment, but the unspoken words weighed like a millstone on his heart.

The damnable bargain they'd struck was proving to be a devil's pact indeed.

* * * * *

Will these two star-crossed lovers find
their sexily-ever-after?
Find out in BOUND TO PLEASE by Hope Tarr,
available in July wherever Harlequin® Blaze™
books are sold.

Silhouette®

SPECIAL EDITION™

NEW YORK TIMES BESTSELLING AUTHOR

DIANA PALMER

A brand-new Long, Tall Texans novel

HEART OF STONE

Feeling unwanted and unloved, Keely returns to Jacobsville and to Boone Sinclair, a rancher troubled by his own past. Boone has always seemed reserved, but now Keely discovers a sensuality with him that quickly turns to love. Can they each see past their own scars to let love in?

Available September 2008 wherever you buy books.

REQUEST YOUR FREE BOOKS!

**2 FREE NOVELS
PLUS 2
FREE GIFTS!**

Passionate, Powerful, Provocative!

HIGH-SOCIETY SECRET PREGNANCY

Park Avenue Scandals

Self-made millionaire Max Rolland had given
up on love until he meets socialite fundraiser
Julia Prentice. After their encounter Julia finds
herself pregnant, but a mysterious blackmailer
threatens to use this surprise pregnancy and ruin
his reputation. Max must decide whether to turn
his back on the woman carrying his child or risk
everything, including his heart....

**Don't miss the next installment of
the Park Avenue Scandals series—
Front Page Engagement
by Laura Wright—
coming in August 2008
from Silhouette Desire!**

Always Powerful, Passionate and Provocative.

COMING NEXT MONTH

**#1879 HIGH-SOCIETY SECRET PREGNANCY—
Maureen Child**
Park Avenue Scandals
With her shocking pregnancy about to be leaked to the press, she
has no choice but to marry the millionaire with whom she spent
one passionate night.

#1880 DANTE'S WEDDING DECEPTION—Day Leclaire
The Dante Legacy
He'd lied and said he was her loving husband. For this Dante
bachelor had to discover the truth behind the woman claiming to
have lost her memory.

#1881 BOUND BY THE KINCAID BABY—Emilie Rose
The Payback Affairs
A will and an orphaned infant had brought them together. Now
they had to decide if passion would tear them apart.

#1882 BILLIONAIRE'S FAVORITE FANTASY—Jan Colley
She'd unknowingly slept with her boss! And now the billionaire
businessman had no intention of letting her get away.

#1883 THE CEO TAKES A WIFE—Maxine Sullivan
With only twelve months to produce an heir it was imperative he
find the perfect bride...no matter what the consequences!

#1884 THE DESERT LORD'S BRIDE—Olivia Gates
Throne of Judar
The marriage had been arranged. And their attraction, unexpected.
But would the heir to the throne choose the crown over the woman
in his bed?

SDCNM0608